I0534326

A Tangled Tale

Lewis Carroll

A Tangled Tale

Copyright © 2021 Bibliotech Press
All rights reserved

The present edition is a reproduction of previous publication of this classic work. Minor typographical errors may have been corrected without note; however, for an authentic reading experience the spelling, punctuation, and capitalization have been retained from the original text.

ISBN: 978-1-63637-424-6

To My Pupil

Beloved pupil! Tamed by thee,
Addish-, Subtrac-, Multiplica-tion,
Division, Fractions, Rule of Three,
Attest thy deft manipulation!

Then onward! Let the voice of Fame
From Age to Age repeat thy story,
Till thou hast won thyself a name
Exceeding even Euclid's glory!

CONTENTS

PREFACE

This Tale originally appeared as a serial in The Monthly Packet, beginning in April, 1880. The writer's intention was to embody in each Knot (like the medicine so dexterously, but ineffectually, concealed in the jam of our early childhood) one or more mathematical questions—in Arithmetic, Algebra, or Geometry, as the case might be—for the amusement, and possible edification, of the fair readers of that Magazine.

L. C.

October, 1885

KNOT I

EXCELSIOR

"Goblin, lead them up and down."

The ruddy glow of sunset was already fading into the sombre shadows of night, when two travellers might have been observed swiftly—at a pace of six miles in the hour—descending the rugged side of a mountain; the younger bounding from crag to crag with the agility of a fawn, while his companion, whose aged limbs seemed ill at ease in the heavy chain armour habitually worn by tourists in that district, toiled on painfully at his side.

As is always the case under such circumstances, the younger knight was the first to break the silence.

"A goodly pace, I trow!" he exclaimed. "We sped not thus in the ascent!"

"Goodly, indeed!" the other echoed with a groan. "We clomb it but at three miles in the hour."

"And on the dead level our pace is——?" the younger suggested; for he was weak in statistics, and left all such details to his aged companion.

"Four miles in the hour," the other wearily replied. "Not an ounce more," he added, with that love of metaphor so common in old age, "and not a farthing less!"

"'Twas three hours past high noon when we left our hostelry," the young man said, musingly. "We shall scarce be back by supper-time. Perchance mine host will roundly deny us all food!"

"He will chide our tardy return," was the grave reply, "and such a rebuke will be meet."

1

"A brave conceit!" cried the other, with a merry laugh. "And should we bid him bring us yet another course, I trow his answer will be tart!"

"We shall but get our deserts," sighed the elder knight, who had never seen a joke in his life, and was somewhat displeased at his companion's untimely levity. "'Twill be nine of the clock," he added in an undertone, "by the time we regain our hostelry. Full many a mile shall we have plodded this day!"

"How many? How many?" cried the eager youth, ever athirst for knowledge.

The old man was silent.

"Tell me," he answered, after a moment's thought, "what time it was when we stood together on yonder peak. Not exact to the minute!" he added hastily, reading a protest in the young man's face. "An' thy guess be within one poor half-hour of the mark, 'tis all I ask of thy mother's son! Then will I tell thee, true to the last inch, how far we shall have trudged betwixt three and nine of the clock."

A groan was the young man's only reply; while his convulsed features and the deep wrinkles that chased each other across his manly brow, revealed the abyss of arithmetical agony into which one chance question had plunged him.

KNOT II

ELIGIBLE APARTMENTS

"Straight down the crooked lane,
And all round the square."

"Let's ask Balbus about it," said Hugh.

"All right," said Lambert.

"He can guess it," said Hugh.

"Rather," said Lambert.

No more words were needed: the two brothers understood each other perfectly.

Balbus was waiting for them at the hotel: the journey down had tired him, he said: so his two pupils had been the round of the place, in search of lodgings, without the old tutor who had been their inseparable companion from their childhood. They had named him after the hero of their Latin exercise-book, which overflowed with anecdotes of that versatile genius—anecdotes whose vagueness in detail was more than compensated by their sensational brilliance. "Balbus has overcome all his enemies" had been marked by their tutor, in the margin of the book, "Successful Bravery." In this way he had tried to extract a moral from every anecdote about Balbus—sometimes one of warning, as in "Balbus had borrowed a healthy dragon," against which he had written "Rashness in Speculation"—sometimes of encouragement, as in the words "Influence of Sympathy in United Action," which stood opposite to the anecdote "Balbus was assisting his mother-in-law to convince the dragon"—and sometimes it dwindled down to a single word, such as "Prudence," which was all he could extract from the touching record that "Balbus, having scorched the tail of the dragon, went away." His pupils liked the short morals best, as it left

3

them more room for marginal illustrations, and in this instance they required all the space they could get to exhibit the rapidity of the hero's departure.

Their report of the state of things was discouraging. That most fashionable of watering-places, Little Mendip, was "chockfull" (as the boys expressed it) from end to end. But in one Square they had seen no less than four cards, in different houses, all announcing in flaming capitals "ELIGIBLE APARTMENTS." "So there's plenty of choice, after all, you see," said spokesman Hugh in conclusion.

"That doesn't follow from the data," said Balbus, as he rose from the easy chair, where he had been dozing over The Little Mendip Gazette. "They may be all single rooms. However, we may as well see them. I shall be glad to stretch my legs a bit."

An unprejudiced bystander might have objected that the operation was needless, and that this long, lank creature would have been all the better with even shorter legs: but no such thought occurred to his loving pupils. One on each side, they did their best to keep up with his gigantic strides, while Hugh repeated the sentence in their father's letter, just received from abroad, over which he and Lambert had been puzzling. "He says a friend of his, the Governor of——what was that name again, Lambert?" ("Kgovjni," said Lambert.) "Well, yes. The Governor of——what-you-may-call-it——wants to give a very small dinner-party, and he means to ask his father's brother-in-law, his brother's father-in-law, his father-in-law's brother, and his brother-in-law's father: and we're to guess how many guests there will be."

There was an anxious pause. "How large did he say the pudding was to be?" Balbus said at last. "Take its cubical contents, divide by the cubical contents of what each man can eat, and the quotient—"

"He didn't say anything about pudding," said Hugh, "—and here's the Square," as they turned a corner and came into sight of the "eligible apartments."

4

"It is a Square!" was Balbus' first cry of delight, as he gazed around him. "Beautiful! Beau-ti-ful! Equilateral! And rectangular!"

The boys looked round with less enthusiasm. "Number nine is the first with a card," said prosaic Lambert; but Balbus would not so soon awake from his dream of beauty.

"See, boys!" he cried. "Twenty doors on a side! What symmetry! Each side divided into twenty-one equal parts! It's delicious!"

"Shall I knock, or ring?" said Hugh, looking in some perplexity at a square brass plate which bore the simple inscription "RING ALSO."

"Both," said Balbus. "That's an Ellipsis, my boy. Did you never see an Ellipsis before?"

"I couldn't hardly read it," said Hugh, evasively. "It's no good having an Ellipsis, if they don't keep it clean."

"Which there is one room, gentlemen," said the smiling landlady. "And a sweet room too! As snug a little back-room——"

"We will see it," said Balbus gloomily, as they followed her in. "I knew how it would be! One room in each house! No view, I suppose?"

"Which indeed there is, gentlemen!" the landlady indignantly protested, as she drew up the blind, and indicated the back garden.

"Cabbages, I perceive," said Balbus. "Well, they're green, at any rate."

"Which the greens at the shops," their hostess explained, "are by no means dependable upon. Here you has them on the premises, and of the best."

"Does the window open?" was always Balbus' first question in testing a lodging: and "Does the chimney smoke?" his second. Satisfied on all points, he secured the refusal of the room, and they moved on to Number Twenty-five.

5

This landlady was grave and stern. "I've nobbut one room left," she told them: "and it gives on the back-gyardin."

"But there are cabbages?" Balbus suggested.

The landlady visibly relented. "There is, sir," she said: "and good ones, though I say it as shouldn't. We can't rely on the shops for greens. So we grows them ourselves."

"A singular advantage," said Balbus: and, after the usual questions, they went on to Fifty-two.

"And I'd gladly accommodate you all, if I could," was the greeting that met them. "We are but mortal," ("Irrelevant!" muttered Balbus) "and I've let all my rooms but one."

"Which one is a back-room, I perceive," said Balbus: "and looking out on—on cabbages, I presume?"

"Yes, indeed, sir!" said their hostess. "Whatever other folks may do, we grows our own. For the shops——"

"An excellent arrangement!" Balbus interrupted. "Then one can really depend on their being good. Does the window open?"

The usual questions were answered satisfactorily: but this time Hugh added one of his own invention—"Does the cat scratch?"

The landlady looked round suspiciously, as if to make sure the cat was not listening, "I will not deceive you, gentlemen," she said. "It do scratch, but not without you pulls its whiskers! It'll never do it," she repeated slowly, with a visible effort to recall the exact words of some written agreement between herself and the cat, "without you pulls its whiskers!"

"Much may be excused in a cat so treated," said Balbus, as they left the house and crossed to Number Seventy-three, leaving the landlady curtseying on the doorstep, and still murmuring to herself her parting words, as if they were a form of blessing, "—— not without you pulls its whiskers!"

At Number Seventy-three they found only a small shy girl to show the house, who said "yes'm" in answer to all questions.

"The usual room," said Balbus, as they marched in: "the usual back-garden, the usual cabbages. I suppose you can't get them good at the shops?"

"Yes'm," said the girl.

"Well, you may tell your mistress we will take the room, and that her plan of growing her own cabbages is simply admirable!"

"Yes'm," said the girl, as she showed them out.

"One day-room and three bed-rooms," said Balbus, as they returned to the hotel. "We will take as our day-room the one that gives us the least walking to do to get to it."

"Must we walk from door to door, and count the steps?" said Lambert.

"No, no! Figure it out, my boys, figure it out!" Balbus gaily exclaimed, as he put pens, ink, and paper before his hapless pupils, and left the room.

"I say! It'll be a job!" said Hugh.

"Rather!" said Lambert.

7

KNOT III

MAD MATHESIS

"I waited for the train."

"Well, they call me so because I am a little mad, I suppose," she said, good-humouredly, in answer to Clara's cautiously-worded question as to how she came by so strange a nick-name. "You see, I never do what sane people are expected to do now-a-days. I never wear long trains, (talking of trains, that's the Charing Cross Metropolitan Station—I've something to tell you about that), and I never play lawn-tennis. I can't cook an omelette. I can't even set a broken limb! There's an ignoramus for you!"

Clara was her niece, and full twenty years her junior; in fact, she was still attending a High School—an institution of which Mad Mathesis spoke with undisguised aversion. "Let a woman be meek and lowly!" she would say. "None of your High Schools for me!" But it was vacation-time just now, and Clara was her guest, and Mad Mathesis was showing her the sights of that Eighth Wonder of the world—London.

"The Charing Cross Metropolitan Station!" she resumed, waving her hand towards the entrance as if she were introducing her niece to a friend. "The Bayswater and Birmingham Extension is just completed, and the trains now run round and round continuously—skirting the border of Wales, just touching at York, and so round by the east coast back to London. The way the trains run is most peculiar. The westerly ones go round in two hours; the easterly ones take three; but they always manage to start two trains from here, opposite ways, punctually every quarter-of-an-hour."

"They part to meet again," said Clara, her eyes filling with tears at the romantic thought.

"No need to cry about it!" her aunt grimly remarked. "They don't meet on the same line of rails, you know. Talking of meeting, an idea strikes me!" she added, changing the subject with her usual abruptness. "Let's go opposite ways round, and see which can meet most trains. No need for a chaperon—ladies' saloon, you know. You shall go whichever way you like, and we'll have a bet about it!"

"I never make bets," Clara said very gravely. "Our excellent preceptress has often warned us——"

"You'd be none the worse if you did!" Mad Mathesis interrupted. "In fact, you'd be the better, I'm certain!"

"Neither does our excellent preceptress approve of puns," said Clara. "But we'll have a match, if you like. Let me choose my train," she added after a brief mental calculation, "and I'll engage to meet exactly half as many again as you do."

"Not if you count fair," Mad Mathesis bluntly interrupted. "Remember, we only count the trains we meet on the way. You mustn't count the one that starts as you start, nor the one that arrives as you arrive."

"That will only make the difference of one train," said Clara, as they turned and entered the station. "But I never travelled alone before. There'll be no one to help me to alight. However, I don't mind. Let's have a match."

A ragged little boy overheard her remark, and came running after her. "Buy a box of cigar-lights, Miss!" he pleaded, pulling her shawl to attract her attention. Clara stopped to explain.

"I never smoke cigars," she said in a meekly apologetic tone. "Our excellent preceptress——," but Mad Mathesis impatiently hurried her on, and the little boy was left gazing after her with round eyes of amazement.

The two ladies bought their tickets and moved slowly down the central platform, Mad Mathesis prattling on as usual—Clara silent, anxiously reconsidering the calculation on which she rested her hopes of winning the match.

"Mind where you go, dear!" cried her aunt, checking her just in time. "One step more, and you'd have been in that pail of cold water!"

"I know, I know," Clara said, dreamily. "The pale, the cold, and the moony——"

"Take your places on the spring-boards!" shouted a porter.

"What are they for!" Clara asked in a terrified whisper.

"Merely to help us into the trains." The elder lady spoke with the nonchalance of one quite used to the process. "Very few people can get into a carriage without help in less than three seconds, and the trains only stop for one second." At this moment the whistle was heard, and two trains rushed into the station. A moment's pause, and they were gone again; but in that brief interval several hundred passengers had been shot into them, each flying straight to his place with the accuracy of a Minie bullet—while an equal number were showered out upon the side-platforms.

Three hours had passed away, and the two friends met again on the Charing Cross platform, and eagerly compared notes. Then Clara turned away with a sigh. To young impulsive hearts, like hers, disappointment is always a bitter pill. Mad Mathesis followed her, full of kindly sympathy.

"Try again, my love!" she said, cheerily. "Let us vary the experiment. We will start as we did before, but not to begin counting till our trains meet. When we see each other, we will say 'One!' and so count on till we come here again."

Clara brightened up. "I shall win that," she exclaimed eagerly, "if I may choose my train!"

Another shriek of engine whistles, another upheaving of spring-boards, another living avalanche plunging into two trains as they flashed by: and the travellers were off again.

Each gazed eagerly from her carriage window, holding up her handkerchief as a signal to her friend. A rush and a roar. Two trains shot past each other in a tunnel, and two travellers leaned back in their corners with a sigh—or rather with two sighs—of relief. "One!" Clara murmured to herself. "Won! It's a word of good omen. This time, at any rate, the victory will be mine!"

But was it?

KNOT IV

THE DEAD RECKONING

"I did dream of money-bags to-night."

Noonday on the open sea within a few degrees of the Equator is apt to be oppressively warm; and our two travellers were now airily clad in suits of dazzling white linen, having laid aside the chain-armour which they had found not only endurable in the cold mountain air they had lately been breathing, but a necessary precaution against the daggers of the banditti who infested the heights. Their holiday-trip was over, and they were now on their way home, in the monthly packet which plied between the two great ports of the island they had been exploring.

Along with their armour, the tourists had laid aside the antiquated speech it had pleased them to affect while in knightly disguise, and had returned to the ordinary style of two country gentlemen of the Twentieth Century.

Stretched on a pile of cushions, under the shade of a huge umbrella, they were lazily watching some native fishermen, who had come on board at the last landing-place, each carrying over his shoulder a small but heavy sack. A large weighing-machine, that had been used for cargo at the last port, stood on the deck; and round this the fishermen had gathered, and, with much unintelligible jabber, seemed to be weighing their sacks.

"More like sparrows in a tree than human talk, isn't it?" the elder tourist remarked to his son, who smiled feebly, but would not exert himself so far as to speak. The old man tried another listener.

"What have they got in those sacks, Captain?" he inquired, as that great being passed them in his never ending parade to and fro on the deck.

12

The Captain paused in his march, and towered over the travellers—tall, grave, and serenely self-satisfied.

"Fishermen," he explained, "are often passengers in My ship. These five are from Mhruxi—the place we last touched at—and that's the way they carry their money. The money of this island is heavy, gentlemen, but it costs little, as you may guess. We buy it from them by weight—about five shillings a pound. I fancy a ten pound-note would buy all those sacks."

By this time the old man had closed his eyes—in order, no doubt, to concentrate his thoughts on these interesting facts; but the Captain failed to realise his motive, and with a grunt resumed his monotonous march.

Meanwhile the fishermen were getting so noisy over the weighing-machine that one of the sailors took the precaution of carrying off all the weights, leaving them to amuse themselves with such substitutes in the form of winch-handles, belaying-pins, &c., as they could find. This brought their excitement to a speedy end: they carefully hid their sacks in the folds of the jib that lay on the deck near the tourists, and strolled away.

When next the Captain's heavy footfall passed, the younger man roused himself to speak.

"What did you call the place those fellows came from, Captain?" he asked.

"Mhruxi, sir."

"And the one we are bound for?"

The Captain took a long breath, plunged into the word, and came out of it nobly. "They call it Kgovjni, sir."

"K—I give it up!" the young man faintly said.

He stretched out his hand for a glass of iced water which the

13

compassionate steward had brought him a minute ago, and had set down, unluckily, just outside the shadow of the umbrella. It was scalding hot, and he decided not to drink it. The effort of making this resolution, coming close on the fatiguing conversation he had just gone through, was too much for him: he sank back among the cushions in silence.

His father courteously tried to make amends for his nonchalance.

"Whereabouts are we now, Captain?" said he, "Have you any idea?"

The Captain cast a pitying look on the ignorant landsman. "I could tell you that, sir," he said, in a tone of lofty condescension, "to an inch!"

"You don't say so!" the old man remarked, in a tone of languid surprise.

"And mean so," persisted the Captain. "Why, what do you suppose would become of My ship, if I were to lose My Longitude and My Latitude? Could you make anything of My Dead Reckoning?"

"Nobody could, I'm sure!" the other heartily rejoined.

But he had overdone it.

"It's perfectly intelligible," the Captain said, in an offended tone, "to any one that understands such things." With these words he moved away, and began giving orders to the men, who were preparing to hoist the jib.

Our tourists watched the operation with such interest that neither of them remembered the five money-bags, which in another moment, as the wind filled out the jib, were whirled overboard and fell heavily into the sea.

But the poor fishermen had not so easily forgotten their property. In a moment they had rushed to the spot, and stood uttering cries of fury, and pointing, now to the sea, and now to the sailors who had caused the disaster.

14

The old man explained it to the Captain.

"Let us make it up among us," he added in conclusion. "Ten pounds will do it, I think you said?"

But the Captain put aside the suggestion with a wave of the hand.

"No, sir!" he said, in his grandest manner. "You will excuse Me, I am sure; but these are My passengers. The accident has happened on board My ship, and under My orders. It is for Me to make compensation." He turned to the angry fishermen. "Come here, my men!" he said, in the Mhruxian dialect. "Tell me the weight of each sack. I saw you weighing them just now."

Then ensued a perfect Babel of noise, as the five natives explained, all screaming together, how the sailors had carried off the weights, and they had done what they could with whatever came handy.

Two iron belaying-pins, three blocks, six holystones, four winch-handles, and a large hammer, were now carefully weighed, the Captain superintending and noting the results. But the matter did not seem to be settled, even then: an angry discussion followed, in which the sailors and the five natives all joined: and at last the Captain approached our tourists with a disconcerted look, which he tried to conceal under a laugh.

"It's an absurd difficulty," he said. "Perhaps one of you gentlemen can suggest something. It seems they weighed the sacks two at a time!"

"If they didn't have five separate weighings, of course you can't value them separately," the youth hastily decided.

"Let's hear all about it," was the old man's more cautious remark.

"They did have five separate weighings," the Captain said, "but— Well, it beats me entirely!" he added, in a sudden burst of candour. "Here's the result. First and second sack weighed twelve pounds; second and third, thirteen and a half; third and fourth, eleven and a

15

half; fourth and fifth, eight: and then they say they had only the large hammer left, and it took three sacks to weigh it down—that's the first, third and fifth—and they weighed sixteen pounds. There, gentlemen! Did you ever hear anything like that?"

The old man muttered under his breath "If only my sister were here!" and looked helplessly at his son. His son looked at the five natives. The five natives looked at the Captain. The Captain looked at nobody: his eyes were cast down, and he seemed to be saying softly to himself "Contemplate one another, gentlemen, if such be your good pleasure. I contemplate Myself!"

KNOT V

OUGHTS AND CROSSES

"Look here, upon this picture, and on this."

"And what made you choose the first train, Goosey?" said Mad Mathesis, as they got into the cab. "Couldn't you count better than that?"

"I took an extreme case," was the tearful reply. "Our excellent preceptress always says 'When in doubt, my dears, take an extreme case.' And I was in doubt."

"Does it always succeed?" her aunt enquired.

Clara sighed. "Not always," she reluctantly admitted. "And I can't make out why. One day she was telling the little girls—they make such a noise at tea, you know—'The more noise you make, the less jam you will have, and vice versâ.' And I thought they wouldn't know what 'vice versâ' meant: so I explained it to them. I said 'If you make an infinite noise, you'll get no jam: and if you make no noise, you'll get an infinite lot of jam.' But our excellent preceptress said that wasn't a good instance. Why wasn't it?" she added plaintively.

Her aunt evaded the question. "One sees certain objections to it," she said. "But how did you work it with the Metropolitan trains? None of them go infinitely fast, I believe."

"I called them hares and tortoises," Clara said—a little timidly, for she dreaded being laughed at. "And I thought there couldn't be so many hares as tortoises on the Line: so I took an extreme case—one hare and an infinite number of tortoises."

"An extreme case, indeed," her aunt remarked with admirable gravity: "and a most dangerous state of things!"

"And I thought, if I went with a tortoise, there would be only one hare to meet: but if I went with the hare—you know there were crowds of tortoises!"

"It wasn't a bad idea," said the elder lady, as they left the cab, at the entrance of Burlington House. "You shall have another chance to-day. We'll have a match in marking pictures."

Clara brightened up. "I should like to try again, very much," she said. "I'll take more care this time. How are we to play?"

To this question Mad Mathesis made no reply: she was busy drawing lines down the margins of the catalogue. "See," she said after a minute, "I've drawn three columns against the names of the pictures in the long room, and I want you to fill them with oughts and crosses—crosses for good marks and oughts for bad. The first column is for choice of subject, the second for arrangement, the third for colouring. And these are the conditions of the match. You must give three crosses to two or three pictures. You must give two crosses to four or five——"

"Do you mean only two crosses?" said Clara. "Or may I count the three-cross pictures among the two-cross pictures?"

"Of course you may," said her aunt. "Any one, that has three eyes, may be said to have two eyes, I suppose?"

Clara followed her aunt's dreamy gaze across the crowded gallery, half-dreading to find that there was a three-eyed person in sight.

"And you must give one cross to nine or ten."

"And which wins the match?" Clara asked, as she carefully entered these conditions on a blank leaf in her catalogue.

"Whichever marks fewest pictures."

"But suppose we marked the same number?"

"Then whichever uses most marks."

18

Clara considered. "I don't think it's much of a match," she said. "I shall mark nine pictures, and give three crosses to three of them, two crosses to two more, and one cross each to all the rest."

"Will you, indeed?" said her aunt. "Wait till you've heard all the conditions, my impetuous child. You must give three oughts to one or two pictures, two oughts to three or four, and one ought to eight or nine. I don't want you to be too hard on the R.A.'s."

Clara quite gasped as she wrote down all these fresh conditions. "It's a great deal worse than Circulating Decimals!" she said. "But I'm determined to win, all the same!"

Her aunt smiled grimly. "We can begin here," she said, as they paused before a gigantic picture, which the catalogue informed them was the "Portrait of Lieutenant Brown, mounted on his favorite elephant."

"He looks awfully conceited!" said Clara. "I don't think he was the elephant's favorite Lieutenant. What a hideous picture it is! And it takes up room enough for twenty!"

"Mind what you say, my dear!" her aunt interposed. "It's by an R.A.!"

But Clara was quite reckless. "I don't care who it's by!" she cried. "And I shall give it three bad marks!"

Aunt and niece soon drifted away from each other in the crowd, and for the next half-hour Clara was hard at work, putting in marks and rubbing them out again, and hunting up and down for suitable pictures. This she found the hardest part of all. "I can't find the one I want!" she exclaimed at last, almost crying with vexation.

"What is it you want to find, my dear?" The voice was strange to Clara, but so sweet and gentle that she felt attracted to the owner of it, even before she had seen her; and when she turned, and met the smiling looks of two little old ladies, whose round dimpled faces, exactly alike, seemed never to have known a care, it was as much as

19

she could do—as she confessed to Aunt Mattie afterwards—to keep herself from hugging them both.

"I was looking for a picture," she said, "that has a good subject—and that's well arranged—but badly coloured."

The little old ladies glanced at each other in some alarm. "Calm yourself, my dear," said the one who had spoken first, "and try to remember which it was. What was the subject?"

"Was it an elephant, for instance?" the other sister suggested. They were still in sight of Lieutenant Brown.

"I don't know, indeed!" Clara impetuously replied. "You know it doesn't matter a bit what the subject is, so long as it's a good one!"

Once more the sisters exchanged looks of alarm, and one of them whispered something to the other, of which Clara caught only the one word "mad."

"They mean Aunt Mattie, of course," she said to herself—fancying, in her innocence, that London was like her native town, where everybody knew everybody else. "If you mean my aunt," she added aloud, "she's there—just three pictures beyond Lieutenant Brown."

"Ah, well! Then you'd better go to her, my dear!" her new friend said, soothingly. "She'll find you the picture you want. Good-bye, dear!"

"Good-bye, dear!" echoed the other sister, "Mind you don't lose sight of your aunt!" And the pair trotted off into another room, leaving Clara rather perplexed at their manner.

"They're real darlings!" she soliloquised. "I wonder why they pity me so!" And she wandered on, murmuring to herself "It must have two good marks, and——"

KNOT VI

HER RADIANCY

"One piecee thing that my have got,
Maskee[1] that thing my no can do.
You talkee you no sabey what?
Bamboo."

They landed, and were at once conducted to the Palace. About half way they were met by the Governor, who welcomed them in English—a great relief to our travellers, whose guide could speak nothing but Kgovjnian.

"I don't half like the way they grin at us as we go by!" the old man whispered to his son. "And why do they say 'Bamboo!' so often?"

"It alludes to a local custom," replied the Governor, who had overheard the question. "Such persons as happen in any way to displease Her Radiancy are usually beaten with rods."

The old man shuddered. "A most objectional local custom!" he remarked with strong emphasis. "I wish we had never landed! Did you notice that black fellow, Norman, opening his great mouth at us? I verily believe he would like to eat us!"

Norman appealed to the Governor, who was walking at his other side. "Do they often eat distinguished strangers here?" he said, in as indifferent a tone as he could assume.

"Not often—not ever!" was the welcome reply. "They are not good for it. Pigs we eat, for they are fat. This old man is thin."

"And thankful to be so!" muttered the elder traveller. "Beaten we shall be without a doubt. It's a comfort to know it won't be Beaten without the B! My dear boy, just look at the peacocks!"

---

[1] "Maskee," in Pigeon-English, means "without."

21

They were now walking between two unbroken lines of those gorgeous birds, each held in check, by means of a golden collar and chain, by a black slave, who stood well behind, so as not to interrupt the view of the glittering tail, with its network of rustling feathers and its hundred eyes.

The Governor smiled proudly. "In your honour," he said, "Her Radiancy has ordered up ten thousand additional peacocks. She will, no doubt, decorate you, before you go, with the usual Star and Feathers."

"It'll be Star without the S!" faltered one of his hearers.

"Come, come! Don't lose heart!" said the other. "All this is full of charm for me."

"You are young, Norman," sighed his father; "young and light-hearted. For me, it is Charm without the C."

"The old one is sad," the Governor remarked with some anxiety. "He has, without doubt, effected some fearful crime?"

"But I haven't!" the poor old gentleman hastily exclaimed. "Tell him I haven't, Norman!"

"He has not, as yet," Norman gently explained. And the Governor repeated, in a satisfied tone, "Not as yet."

"Yours is a wondrous country!" the Governor resumed, after a pause. "Now here is a letter from a friend of mine, a merchant, in London. He and his brother went there a year ago, with a thousand pounds apiece; and on New-Year's-day they had sixty thousand pounds between them!"

"How did they do it?" Norman eagerly exclaimed. Even the elder traveller looked excited.

The Governor handed him the open letter. "Anybody can do it, when once they know how," so ran this oracular document. "We borrowed nought: we stole nought. We began the year with only a thousand pounds apiece: and last New-Year's-day we had sixty thousand pounds between us—sixty thousand golden sovereigns!"

Norman looked grave and thoughtful as he handed back the letter. His father hazarded one guess. "Was it by gambling?"

"A Kgovjnian never gambles," said the Governor gravely, as he ushered them through the palace gates. They followed him in silence down a long passage, and soon found themselves in a lofty hall, lined entirely with peacocks' feathers. In the centre was a pile of crimson cushions, which almost concealed the figure of Her Radiancy—a plump little damsel, in a robe of green satin dotted with silver stars, whose pale round face lit up for a moment with a half-smile as the travellers bowed before her, and then relapsed into the exact expression of a wax doll, while she languidly murmured a word or two in the Kgovjnian dialect.

The Governor interpreted. "Her Radiancy welcomes you. She notes the Impenetrable Placidity of the old one, and the Imperceptible Acuteness of the youth."

Here the little potentate clapped her hands, and a troop of slaves instantly appeared, carrying trays of coffee and sweetmeats, which they offered to the guests, who had, at a signal from the Governor, seated themselves on the carpet.

"Sugar-plums!" muttered the old man. "One might as well be at a confectioner's! Ask for a penny bun, Norman!"

"Not so loud!" his son whispered. "Say something complimentary!" For the Governor was evidently expecting a speech.

"We thank Her Exalted Potency," the old man timidly began. "We bask in the light of her smile, which——"

"The words of old men are weak!" the Governor interrupted angrily. "Let the youth speak!"

23

"Tell her," cried Norman, in a wild burst of eloquence, "that, like two grasshoppers in a volcano, we are shrivelled up in the presence of Her Spangled Vehemence!"

"It is well," said the Governor, and translated this into Kgovjnian. "I am now to tell you," he proceeded, "what Her Radiancy requires of you before you go. The yearly competition for the post of Imperial Scarf-maker is just ended; you are the judges. You will take account of the rate of work, the lightness of the scarves, and their warmth. Usually the competitors differ in one point only. Thus, last year, Fifi and Gogo made the same number of scarves in the trial-week, and they were equally light; but Fifi's were twice as warm as Gogo's and she was pronounced twice as good. But this year, woe is me, who can judge it? Three competitors are here, and they differ in all points! While you settle their claims, you shall be lodged, Her Radiancy bids me say, free of expense—in the best dungeon, and abundantly fed on the best bread and water."

The old man groaned. "All is lost!" he wildly exclaimed. But Norman heeded him not: he had taken out his note-book, and was calmly jotting down the particulars.

"Three they be," the Governor proceeded, "Lolo, Mimi, and Zuzu. Lolo makes 5 scarves while Mimi makes 2; but Zuzu makes 4 while Lolo makes 3! Again, so fairylike is Zuzu's handiwork, 5 of her scarves weigh no more than one of Lolo's; yet Mimi's is lighter still—5 of hers will but balance 3 of Zuzu's! And for warmth one of Mimi's is equal to 4 of Zuzu's; yet one of Lolo's is as warm as 3 of Mimi's!"

Here the little lady once more clapped her hands.

"It is our signal of dismissal!" the Governor hastily said. "Pay Her Radiancy your farewell compliments—and walk out backwards."

The walking part was all the elder tourist could manage. Norman simply said "Tell Her Radiancy we are transfixed by the spectacle of

Her Serene Brilliance, and bid an agonized farewell to her Condensed Milkiness!"

"Her Radiancy is pleased," the Governor reported, after duly translating this. "She casts on you a glance from Her Imperial Eyes, and is confident that you will catch it!"

"That I warrant we shall!" the elder traveller moaned to himself distractedly.

Once more they bowed low, and then followed the Governor down a winding staircase to the Imperial Dungeon, which they found to be lined with coloured marble, lighted from the roof, and splendidly though not luxuriously furnished with a bench of polished malachite. "I trust you will not delay the calculation," the Governor said, ushering them in with much ceremony. "I have known great inconvenience—great and serious inconvenience—result to those unhappy ones who have delayed to execute the commands of Her Radiancy! And on this occasion she is resolute: she says the thing must and shall be done: and she has ordered up ten thousand additional bamboos!" With these words he left them, and they heard him lock and bar the door on the outside.

"I told you how it would end!" moaned the elder traveller, wringing his hands, and quite forgetting in his anguish that he had himself proposed the expedition, and had never predicted anything of the sort. "Oh that we were well out of this miserable business!"

"Courage!" cried the younger cheerily. "Hæc olim meminisse juvabit! The end of all this will be glory!"

"Glory without the L!" was all the poor old man could say, as he rocked himself to and fro on the malachite bench. "Glory without the L!"

25

KNOT VII

PETTY CASH

"Base is the slave that pays."

"Aunt Mattie!"

"My child?"

"Would you mind writing it down at once? I shall be quite certain to forget it if you don't!"

"My dear, we really must wait till the cab stops. How can I possibly write anything in the midst of all this jolting?"

"But really I shall be forgetting it!"

Clara's voice took the plaintive tone that her aunt never knew how to resist, and with a sigh the old lady drew forth her ivory tablets and prepared to record the amount that Clara had just spent at the confectioner's shop. Her expenditure was always made out of her aunt's purse, but the poor girl knew, by bitter experience, that sooner or later "Mad Mathesis" would expect an exact account of every penny that had gone, and she waited, with ill-concealed impatience, while the old lady turned the tablets over and over, till she had found the one headed "PETTY CASH."

"Here's the place," she said at last, "and here we have yesterday's luncheon duly entered. One glass lemonade (Why can't you drink water, like me?) three sandwiches (They never put in half mustard enough. I told the young woman so, to her face; and she tossed her head—like her impudence!) and seven biscuits. Total one-and-two-pence. Well, now for to-day's?"

"One glass of lemonade——" Clara was beginning to say, when suddenly the cab drew up, and a courteous railway-porter was handing out the bewildered girl before she had had time to finish her sentence.

Her aunt pocketed the tablets instantly. "Business first," she said: "petty cash—which is a form of pleasure, whatever you may think—afterwards." And she proceeded to pay the driver, and to give voluminous orders about the luggage, quite deaf to the entreaties of her unhappy niece that she would enter the rest of the luncheon account. "My dear, you really must cultivate a more capacious mind!" was all the consolation she vouchsafed to the poor girl. "Are not the tablets of your memory wide enough to contain the record of one single luncheon?"

"Not wide enough! Not half wide enough!" was the passionate reply.

The words came in aptly enough, but the voice was not that of Clara, and both ladies turned in some surprise to see who it was that had so suddenly struck into their conversation. A fat little old lady was standing at the door of a cab, helping the driver to extricate what seemed an exact duplicate of herself: it would have been no easy task to decide which was the fatter, or which looked the more good-humoured of the two sisters.

"I tell you the cab-door isn't half wide enough!" she repeated, as her sister finally emerged, somewhat after the fashion of a pellet from a pop-gun, and she turned to appeal to Clara. "Is it, dear?" she said, trying hard to bring a frown into a face that dimpled all over with smiles.

"Some folks is too wide for 'em," growled the cab-driver.

"Don't provoke me, man!" cried the little old lady, in what she meant for a tempest of fury. "Say another word and I'll put you into the County Court, and sue you for a Habeas Corpus!" The cabman touched his hat, and marched off, grinning.

"Nothing like a little Law to cow the ruffians, my dear!" she

27

remarked confidentially to Clara. "You saw how he quailed when I mentioned the Habeas Corpus? Not that I've any idea what it means, but it sounds very grand, doesn't it?"

"It's very provoking," Clara replied, a little vaguely.

"Very!" the little old lady eagerly repeated. "And we're very much provoked indeed. Aren't we, sister?"

"I never was so provoked in all my life!" the fatter sister assented, radiantly.

By this time Clara had recognised her picture-gallery acquaintances, and, drawing her aunt aside, she hastily whispered her reminiscences. "I met them first in the Royal Academy—and they were very kind to me—and they were lunching at the next table to us, just now, you know—and they tried to help me to find the picture I wanted—and I'm sure they're dear old things!"

"Friends of yours, are they?" said Mad Mathesis. "Well, I like their looks. You can be civil to them, while I get the tickets. But do try and arrange your ideas a little more chronologically!"

And so it came to pass that the four ladies found themselves seated side by side on the same bench waiting for the train, and chatting as if they had known one another for years.

"Now this I call quite a remarkable coincidence!" exclaimed the smaller and more talkative of the two sisters—the one whose legal knowledge had annihilated the cab-driver. "Not only that we should be waiting for the same train, and at the same station—that would be curious enough—but actually on the same day, and the same hour of the day! That's what strikes me so forcibly!" She glanced at the fatter and more silent sister, whose chief function in life seemed to be to support the family opinion, and who meekly responded—

"And me too, sister!"

"Those are not independent coincidences——" Mad Mathesis was just beginning, when Clara ventured to interpose.

"There's no jolting here," she pleaded meekly. "Would you mind writing it down now?"

Out came the ivory tablets once more. "What was it, then?" said her aunt.

"One glass of lemonade, one sandwich, one biscuit—Oh dear me!" cried poor Clara, the historical tone suddenly changing to a wail of agony.

"Toothache?" said her aunt calmly, as she wrote down the items. The two sisters instantly opened their reticules and produced two different remedies for neuralgia, each marked "unequalled."

"It isn't that!" said poor Clara. "Thank you very much. It's only that I can't remember how much I paid!"

"Well, try and make it out, then," said her aunt. "You've got yesterday's luncheon to help you, you know. And here's the luncheon we had the day before—the first day we went to that shop—one glass lemonade, four sandwiches, ten biscuits. Total, one-and-fivepence." She handed the tablets to Clara, who gazed at them with eyes so dim with tears that she did not at first notice that she was holding them upside down.

The two sisters had been listening to all this with the deepest interest, and at this juncture the smaller one softly laid her hand on Clara's arm.

"Do you know, my dear," she said coaxingly, "my sister and I are in the very same predicament! Quite identically the very same predicament! Aren't we, sister?"

"Quite identically and absolutely the very——" began the fatter sister, but she was constructing her sentence on too large a scale, and the little one would not wait for her to finish it.

"Yes, my dear," she resumed; "we were lunching at the very same shop as you were—and we had two glasses of lemonade and three sandwiches and five biscuits—and neither of us has the least idea what we paid. Have we, sister?"

"Quite identically and absolutely——" murmured the other, who evidently considered that she was now a whole sentence in arrears, and that she ought to discharge one obligation before contracting any fresh liabilities; but the little lady broke in again, and she retired from the conversation a bankrupt.

"Would you make it out for us, my dear?" pleaded the little old lady.

"You can do Arithmetic, I trust?" her aunt said, a little anxiously, as Clara turned from one tablet to another, vainly trying to collect her thoughts. Her mind was a blank, and all human expression was rapidly fading out of her face.

A gloomy silence ensued.

KNOT VIII

DE OMNIBUS REBUS

"This little pig went to market:
This little pig staid at home."

"By Her Radiancy's express command," said the Governor, as he conducted the travellers, for the last time, from the Imperial presence, "I shall now have the ecstasy of escorting you as far as the outer gate of the Military Quarter, where the agony of parting—if indeed Nature can survive the shock—must be endured! From that gate grurmstipths start every quarter of an hour, both ways——"

"Would you mind repeating that word?" said Norman. "Grurm—?"

"Grurmstipths," the Governor repeated. "You call them omnibuses in England. They run both ways, and you can travel by one of them all the way down to the harbour."

The old man breathed a sigh of relief; four hours of courtly ceremony had wearied him, and he had been in constant terror lest something should call into use the ten thousand additional bamboos.

In another minute they were crossing a large quadrangle, paved with marble, and tastefully decorated with a pigsty in each corner. Soldiers, carrying pigs, were marching in all directions: and in the middle stood a gigantic officer giving orders in a voice of thunder, which made itself heard above all the uproar of the pigs.

"It is the Commander-in-Chief!" the Governor hurriedly whispered to his companions, who at once followed his example in prostrating themselves before the great man. The Commander gravely bowed in return. He was covered with gold lace from head to foot: his face wore an expression of deep misery: and he had a little black pig under each arm. Still the gallant fellow did his best, in the midst of

31

the orders he was every moment issuing to his men, to bid a courteous farewell to the departing guests.

"Farewell, oh old one—carry these three to the South corner—and farewell to thee, thou young one—put this fat one on the top of the others in the Western sty—may your shadows never be less—woe is me, it is wrongly done! Empty out all the sties, and begin again!" And the soldier leant upon his sword, and wiped away a tear.

"He is in distress," the Governor explained as they left the court. "Her Radiancy has commanded him to place twenty-four pigs in those four sties, so that, as she goes round the court, she may always find the number in each sty nearer to ten than the number in the last."

"Does she call ten nearer to ten than nine is?" said Norman.

"Surely," said the Governor. "Her Radiancy would admit that ten is nearer to ten than nine is—and also nearer than eleven is."

"Then I think it can be done," said Norman.

The Governor shook his head. "The Commander has been transferring them in vain for four months," he said. "What hope remains? And Her Radiancy has ordered up ten thousand additional——"

"The pigs don't seem to enjoy being transferred," the old man hastily interrupted. He did not like the subject of bamboos.

"They are only provisionally transferred, you know," said the Governor. "In most cases they are immediately carried back again: so they need not mind it. And all is done with the greatest care, under the personal superintendence of the Commander-in-Chief."

"Of course she would only go once round?" said Norman.

"Alas, no!" sighed their conductor. "Round and round. Round and round. These are Her Radiancy's own words. But oh, agony! Here is the outer gate, and we must part!" He sobbed as he shook hands with them, and the next moment was briskly walking away.

"He might have waited to see us off!" said the old man, piteously.

"And he needn't have begun whistling the very moment he left us!" said the young one, severely. "But look sharp—here are two what's-his-names in the act of starting!"

Unluckily, the sea-bound omnibus was full. "Never mind!" said Norman, cheerily. "We'll walk on till the next one overtakes us."

They trudged on in silence, both thinking over the military problem, till they met an omnibus coming from the sea. The elder traveller took out his watch. "Just twelve minutes and a half since we started," he remarked in an absent manner. Suddenly the vacant face brightened; the old man had an idea. "My boy!" he shouted, bringing his hand down upon Norman's shoulder so suddenly as for a moment to transfer his centre of gravity beyond the base of support.

Thus taken off his guard, the young man wildly staggered forwards, and seemed about to plunge into space: but in another moment he had gracefully recovered himself. "Problem in Precession and Nutation," he remarked—in tones where filial respect only just managed to conceal a shade of annoyance. "What is it?" he hastily added, fearing his father might have been taken ill. "Will you have some brandy?"

"When will the next omnibus overtake us? When? When?" the old man cried, growing more excited every moment.

Norman looked gloomy. "Give me time," he said. "I must think it over." And once more the travellers passed on in silence—a silence only broken by the distant squeals of the unfortunate little pigs, who were still being provisionally transferred from sty to sty, under the personal superintendence of the Commander-in-Chief.

KNOT IX

A SERPENT WITH CORNERS

"Water, water, every where,
Nor any drop to drink."

"It'll just take one more pebble."

"What ever are you doing with those buckets?"

The speakers were Hugh and Lambert. Place, the beach of Little Mendip. Time, 1.30, P.M. Hugh was floating a bucket in another a size larger, and trying how many pebbles it would carry without sinking. Lambert was lying on his back, doing nothing.

For the next minute or two Hugh was silent, evidently deep in thought. Suddenly he started. "I say, look here, Lambert!" he cried.

"If it's alive, and slimy, and with legs, I don't care to," said Lambert.

"Didn't Balbus say this morning that, if a body is immersed in liquid, it displaces as much liquid as is equal to its own bulk?" said Hugh.

"He said things of that sort," Lambert vaguely replied.

"Well, just look here a minute. Here's the little bucket almost quite immersed: so the water displaced ought to be just about the same bulk. And now just look at it!" He took out the little bucket as he spoke, and handed the big one to Lambert. "Why, there's hardly a teacupful! Do you mean to say that water is the same bulk as the little bucket?"

"Course it is," said Lambert.

"Well, look here again!" cried Hugh, triumphantly, as he poured the water from the big bucket into the little one. "Why, it doesn't half fill it!"

34

"That's its business," said Lambert. "If Balbus says it's the same bulk, why, it is the same bulk, you know."

"Well, I don't believe it," said Hugh.

"You needn't," said Lambert. "Besides, it's dinner-time. Come along."

They found Balbus waiting dinner for them, and to him Hugh at once propounded his difficulty.

"Let's get you helped first," said Balbus, briskly cutting away at the joint. "You know the old proverb 'Mutton first, mechanics afterwards'?"

The boys did not know the proverb, but they accepted it in perfect good faith, as they did every piece of information, however startling, that came from so infallible an authority as their tutor. They ate on steadily in silence, and, when dinner was over, Hugh set out the usual array of pens, ink, and paper, while Balbus repeated to them the problem he had prepared for their afternoon's task.

"A friend of mine has a flower-garden—a very pretty one, though no great size—"

"How big is it?" said Hugh.

"That's what you have to find out!" Balbus gaily replied. "All I tell you is that it is oblong in shape—just half a yard longer than its width—and that a gravel-walk, one yard wide, begins at one corner and runs all round it."

"Joining into itself?" said Hugh.

"Not joining into itself, young man. Just before doing that, it turns a corner, and runs round the garden again, alongside of the first portion, and then inside that again, winding in and in, and each lap touching the last one, till it has used up the whole of the area."

"Like a serpent with corners?" said Lambert.

"Exactly so. And if you walk the whole length of it, to the last inch, keeping in the centre of the path, it's exactly two miles and half a furlong. Now, while you find out the length and breadth of the garden, I'll see if I can think out that sea-water puzzle."

"You said it was a flower-garden?" Hugh inquired, as Balbus was leaving the room.

"I did," said Balbus.

"Where do the flowers grow?" said Hugh. But Balbus thought it best not to hear the question. He left the boys to their problem, and, in the silence of his own room, set himself to unravel Hugh's mechanical paradox.

"To fix our thoughts," he murmured to himself, as, with hands deep-buried in his pockets, he paced up and down the room, "we will take a cylindrical glass jar, with a scale of inches marked up the side, and fill it with water up to the 10-inch mark: and we will assume that every inch depth of jar contains a pint of water. We will now take a solid cylinder, such that every inch of it is equal in bulk to half a pint of water, and plunge 4 inches of it into the water, so that the end of the cylinder comes down to the 6-inch mark. Well, that displaces 2 pints of water. What becomes of them? Why, if there were no more cylinder, they would lie comfortably on the top, and fill the jar up to the 12-inch mark. But unfortunately there is more cylinder, occupying half the space between the 10-inch and the 12-inch marks, so that only one pint of water can be accommodated there. What becomes of the other pint? Why, if there were no more cylinder, it would lie on the top, and fill the jar up to the 13-inch mark. But unfortunately— —Shade of Newton!" he exclaimed, in sudden accents of terror. "When does the water stop rising?"

A bright idea struck him. "I'll write a little essay on it," he said.

36

"When a solid is immersed in a liquid, it is well known that it displaces a portion of the liquid equal to itself in bulk, and that the level of the liquid rises just so much as it would rise if a quantity of liquid had been added to it, equal in bulk to the solid. Lardner says, precisely the same process occurs when a solid is partially immersed: the quantity of liquid displaced, in this case, equalling the portion of the solid which is immersed, and the rise of the level being in proportion.

"Suppose a solid held above the surface of a liquid and partially immersed: a portion of the liquid is displaced, and the level of the liquid rises. But, by this rise of level, a little bit more of the solid is of course immersed, and so there is a new displacement of a second portion of the liquid, and a consequent rise of level. Again, this second rise of level causes a yet further immersion, and by consequence another displacement of liquid and another rise. It is self-evident that this process must continue till the entire solid is immersed, and that the liquid will then begin to immerse whatever holds the solid, which, being connected with it, must for the time be considered a part of it. If you hold a stick, six feet long, with its end in a tumbler of water, and wait long enough, you must eventually be immersed. The question as to the source from which the water is supplied—which belongs to a high branch of mathematics, and is therefore beyond our present scope—does not apply to the sea. Let us therefore take the familiar instance of a man standing at the edge of the sea, at ebb-tide, with a solid in his hand, which he partially immerses: he remains steadfast and unmoved, and we all know that he must be drowned. The multitudes who daily perish in this manner to attest a philosophical truth, and whose bodies the unreasoning wave casts sullenly upon our thankless shores, have a truer claim to be called the martyrs of science than a Galileo or a Kepler. To use Kossuth's eloquent phrase, they are the unnamed demigods of the nineteenth century."[2]

---

[2] Note by the writer.—For the above Essay I am indebted to a dear friend, now deceased.

"There's a fallacy somewhere," he murmured drowsily, as he stretched his long legs upon the sofa. "I must think it over again." He closed his eyes, in order to concentrate his attention more perfectly, and for the next hour or so his slow and regular breathing bore witness to the careful deliberation with which he was investigating this new and perplexing view of the subject.

KNOT X

CHELSEA BUNS

"Yea, buns, and buns, and buns!"
Old Song.

"How very, very sad!" exclaimed Clara; and the eyes of the gentle girl filled with tears as she spoke.

"Sad—but very curious when you come to look at it arithmetically," was her aunt's less romantic reply. "Some of them have lost an arm in their country's service, some a leg, some an ear, some an eye——"

"And some, perhaps, all!" Clara murmured dreamily, as they passed the long rows of weather-beaten heroes basking in the sun. "Did you notice that very old one, with a red face, who was drawing a map in the dust with his wooden leg, and all the others watching? I think it was a plan of a battle——"

"The battle of Trafalgar, no doubt," her aunt interrupted, briskly.

"Hardly that, I think," Clara ventured to say. "You see, in that case, he couldn't well be alive——"

"Couldn't well be alive!" the old lady contemptuously repeated. "He's as lively as you and me put together! Why, if drawing a map in the dust—with one's wooden leg—doesn't prove one to be alive, perhaps you'll kindly mention what does prove it!"

Clara did not see her way out of it. Logic had never been her forte.

"To return to the arithmetic," Mad Mathesis resumed—the eccentric old lady never let slip an opportunity of driving her niece into a calculation—"what percentage do you suppose must have lost all four—a leg, an arm, an eye, and an ear?"

39

"How can I tell?" gasped the terrified girl. She knew well what was coming.

"You can't, of course, without data," her aunt replied: "but I'm just going to give you— —"

"Give her a Chelsea bun, Miss! That's what most young ladies likes best!" The voice was rich and musical, and the speaker dexterously whipped back the snowy cloth that covered his basket, and disclosed a tempting array of the familiar square buns, joined together in rows, richly egged and browned, and glistening in the sun.

"No, sir! I shall give her nothing so indigestible! Be off!" The old lady waved her parasol threateningly: but nothing seemed to disturb the good-humour of the jolly old man, who marched on, chanting his melodious refrain:—

"Far too indigestible, my love!" said the old lady. "Percentages will agree with you ever so much better!"

Clara sighed, and there was a hungry look in her eyes as she watched the basket lessening in the distance: but she meekly listened to the relentless old lady, who at once proceeded to count off the data on her fingers.

"Say that 70 per cent. have lost an eye—75 per cent. an ear—80 per cent. an arm—85 per cent. a leg—that'll do it beautifully. Now, my dear, what percentage, at least, must have lost all four?"

No more conversation occurred—unless a smothered exclamation of "Piping hot!" which escaped from Clara's lips as the basket vanished round a corner could be counted as such—until they reached the old Chelsea mansion, where Clara's father was then staying, with his three sons and their old tutor.

Balbus, Lambert, and Hugh had entered the house only a few minutes before them. They had been out walking, and Hugh had been propounding a difficulty which had reduced Lambert to the depths of gloom, and had even puzzled Balbus.

"It changes from Wednesday to Thursday at midnight, doesn't it?" Hugh had begun.

"Sometimes," said Balbus, cautiously.

"Always," said Lambert, decisively.

"Sometimes," Balbus gently insisted. "Six midnights out of seven, it changes to some other name."

"I meant, of course," Hugh corrected himself, "when it does change from Wednesday to Thursday, it does it at midnight—and only at midnight."

"Surely," said Balbus. Lambert was silent.

"Well, now, suppose it's midnight here in Chelsea. Then it's Wednesday west of Chelsea (say in Ireland or America) where midnight hasn't arrived yet: and it's Thursday east of Chelsea (say in Germany or Russia) where midnight has just passed by?"

"Surely," Balbus said again. Even Lambert nodded this time.

"But it isn't midnight, anywhere else; so it can't be changing from one day to another anywhere else. And yet, if Ireland and America and so on call it Wednesday, and Germany and Russia and so on call it Thursday, there must be some place—not Chelsea—that has different days on the two sides of it. And the worst of it is, the people there get their days in the wrong order: they've got

41

Wednesday east of them, and Thursday west—just as if their day had changed from Thursday to Wednesday!"

"I've heard that puzzle before!" cried Lambert. "And I'll tell you the explanation. When a ship goes round the world from east to west, we know that it loses a day in its reckoning: so that when it gets home, and calls its day Wednesday, it finds people here calling it Thursday, because we've had one more midnight than the ship has had. And when you go the other way round you gain a day."

"I know all that," said Hugh, in reply to this not very lucid explanation: "but it doesn't help me, because the ship hasn't proper days. One way round, you get more than twenty-four hours to the day, and the other way you get less: so of course the names get wrong: but people that live on in one place always get twenty-four hours to the day."

"I suppose there is such a place," Balbus said, meditatively, "though I never heard of it. And the people must find it very queer, as Hugh says, to have the old day east of them, and the new one west: because, when midnight comes round to them, with the new day in front of it and the old one behind it, one doesn't see exactly what happens. I must think it over."

So they had entered the house in the state I have described—Balbus puzzled, and Lambert buried in gloomy thought.

"Yes, m'm, Master is at home, m'm," said the stately old butler. (N.B.—It is only a butler of experience who can manage a series of three M's together, without any interjacent vowels.) "And the ole party is a-waiting for you in the libery."

"I don't like his calling your father an old party," Mad Mathesis whispered to her niece, as they crossed the hall. And Clara had only just time to whisper in reply "he meant the whole party," before they were ushered into the library, and the sight of the five solemn faces there assembled chilled her into silence.

42

Her father sat at the head of the table, and mutely signed to the ladies to take the two vacant chairs, one on each side of him. His three sons and Balbus completed the party. Writing materials had been arranged round the table, after the fashion of a ghostly banquet: the butler had evidently bestowed much thought on the grim device. Sheets of quarto paper, each flanked by a pen on one side and a pencil on the other, represented the plates—penwipers did duty for rolls of bread—while ink-bottles stood in the places usually occupied by wine-glasses. The pièce de resistance was a large green baize bag, which gave forth, as the old man restlessly lifted it from side to side, a charming jingle, as of innumerable golden guineas.

"Sister, daughter, sons—and Balbus—," the old man began, so nervously, that Balbus put in a gentle "Hear, hear!" while Hugh drummed on the table with his fists. This disconcerted the unpractised orator. "Sister—" he began again, then paused a moment, moved the bag to the other side, and went on with a rush, "I mean—this being—a critical occasion—more or less—being the year when one of my sons comes of age—" he paused again in some confusion, having evidently got into the middle of his speech sooner than he intended: but it was too late to go back. "Hear, hear!" cried Balbus. "Quite so," said the old gentleman, recovering his self-possession a little: "when first I began this annual custom—my friend Balbus will correct me if I am wrong—" (Hugh whispered "with a strap!" but nobody heard him except Lambert, who only frowned and shook his head at him) "—this annual custom of giving each of my sons as many guineas as would represent his age—it was a critical time—so Balbus informed me—as the ages of two of you were together equal to that of the third—so on that occasion I made a speech——" He paused so long that Balbus thought it well to come to the rescue with the words "It was a most——" but the old man checked him with a warning look: "yes, made a speech," he repeated. "A few years after that, Balbus pointed out—I say pointed out—" ("Hear, hear"! cried Balbus. "Quite so," said the grateful old man.) "—that it was another critical

43

occasion. The ages of two of you were together double that of the third. So I made another speech—another speech. And now again it's a critical occasion—so Balbus says—and I am making——" (Here Mad Mathesis pointedly referred to her watch) "all the haste I can!" the old man cried, with wonderful presence of mind. "Indeed, sister, I'm coming to the point now! The number of years that have passed since that first occasion is just two-thirds of the number of guineas I then gave you. Now, my boys, calculate your ages from the data, and you shall have the money!"

"But we know our ages!" cried Hugh.

"Silence, sir!" thundered the old man, rising to his full height (he was exactly five-foot five) in his indignation. "I say you must use the data only! You mustn't even assume which it is that comes of age!" He clutched the bag as he spoke, and with tottering steps (it was about as much as he could do to carry it) he left the room.

"And you shall have a similar cadeau," the old lady whispered to her niece, "when you've calculated that percentage!" And she followed her brother.

Nothing could exceed the solemnity with which the old couple had risen from the table, and yet was it—was it a grin with which the father turned away from his unhappy sons? Could it be—could it be a wink with which the aunt abandoned her despairing niece? And were those—were those sounds of suppressed chuckling which floated into the room, just before Balbus (who had followed them out) closed the door? Surely not: and yet the butler told the cook—but no, that was merely idle gossip, and I will not repeat it.

The shades of evening granted their unuttered petition, and "closed not o'er" them (for the butler brought in the lamp): the same obliging shades left them a "lonely bark" (the wail of a dog, in the back-yard, baying the moon) for "awhile": but neither "morn, alas," (nor any other epoch) seemed likely to "restore" them—to that peace of mind which had once been theirs ere ever these problems had swooped upon them, and crushed them with a load of unfathomable mystery!

"It's hardly fair," muttered Hugh, "to give us such a jumble as this to work out!"

"Fair?" Clara echoed, bitterly. "Well!"

And to all my readers I can but repeat the last words of gentle Clara—

Fare-well!

45

APPENDIX

"A knot!" said Alice. "Oh, do let me help to undo it!"

ANSWERS TO KNOT I

Problem.—"Two travellers spend from 3 o'clock till 9 in walking along a level road, up a hill, and home again: their pace on the level being 4 miles an hour, up hill 3, and down hill 6. Find distance walked: also (within half an hour) time of reaching top of hill."

Answer.—"24 miles: half-past 6."

Solution.—A level mile takes ¼ of an hour, up hill 1/3, down hill 1/6. Hence to go and return over the same mile, whether on the level or on the hill-side, takes ½ an hour. Hence in 6 hours they went 12 miles out and 12 back. If the 12 miles out had been nearly all level, they would have taken a little over 3 hours; if nearly all up hill, a little under 4. Hence 3½ hours must be within ½ an hour of the time taken in reaching the peak; thus, as they started at 3, they got there within ½ an hour of ½ past 6.

Twenty-seven answers have come in. Of these, 9 are right, 16 partially right, and 2 wrong. The 16 give the distance correctly, but they have failed to grasp the fact that the top of the hill might have been reached at any moment between 6 o'clock and 7.

The two wrong answers are from Gerty Vernon and A Nihilist. The former makes the distance "23 miles," while her revolutionary companion puts it at "27." Gerty Vernon says "they had to go 4 miles along the plain, and got to the foot of the hill at 4 o'clock." They might have done so, I grant; but you have no ground for saying they did so. "It was 7½ miles to the top of the hill, and they reached that at ¼ before 7 o'clock." Here you go wrong in your

46

arithmetic, and I must, however reluctantly, bid you farewell. 7½ miles, at 3 miles an hour, would not require 2¾ hours. A Nihilist says "Let x denote the whole number of miles; y the number of hours to hill-top; ∴ 3y = number of miles to hill-top, and x-3y = number of miles on the other side." You bewilder me. The other side of what? "Of the hill," you say. But then, how did they get home again? However, to accommodate your views we will build a new hostelry at the foot of the hill on the opposite side, and also assume (what I grant you is possible, though it is not necessarily true) that there was no level road at all. Even then you go wrong.

You say

$$"y = 6 - (x - 3y)/6, \qquad ..... (i);$$

$$x/4½ = 6 \qquad ..... (ii)."$$

I grant you (i), but I deny (ii): it rests on the assumption that to go part of the time at 3 miles an hour, and the rest at 6 miles an hour, comes to the same result as going the whole time at 4½ miles an hour. But this would only be true if the "part" were an exact half, i.e., if they went up hill for 3 hours, and down hill for the other 3: which they certainly did not do.

The sixteen, who are partially right, are Agnes Bailey, F. K., Fifee, G. E. B., H. P., Kit, M. E. T., Mysie, A Mother's Son, Nairam, A Redruthian, A Socialist, Spear Maiden, T. B. C., Vis Inertiæ, and Yak. Of these, F. K., Fifee, T. B. C., and Vis Inertiæ do not attempt the second part at all. F. K. and H. P. give no working. The rest make particular assumptions, such as that there was no level road — that there were 6 miles of level road — and so on, all leading to particular times being fixed for reaching the hill-top. The most curious assumption is that of Agnes Bailey, who says "Let x = number of hours occupied in ascent; then x/2 = hours occupied in descent; and 4x/3 = hours occupied on the level." I suppose you were thinking of the relative rates, up hill and on the level; which we might express by saying that, if they went x miles up hill in a certain time, they would go 4x/3 miles on the level in the same time.

You have, in fact, assumed that they took the same time on the level that they took in ascending the hill. Fifee assumes that, when the aged knight said they had gone "four miles in the hour" on the level, he meant that four miles was the distance gone, not merely the rate. This would have been—if Fifee will excuse the slang expression—a "sell," ill-suited to the dignity of the hero.

And now "descend, ye classic Nine!" who have solved the whole problem, and let me sing your praises. Your names are Blithe, E. W., L. B., A Marlborough Boy, O. V. L., Putney Walker, Rose, Sea Breeze, Simple Susan, and Money Spinner. (These last two I count as one, as they send a joint answer.) Rose and Simple Susan and Co. do not actually state that the hill-top was reached some time between 6 and 7, but, as they have clearly grasped the fact that a mile, ascended and descended, took the same time as two level miles, I mark them as "right." A Marlborough Boy and Putney Walker deserve honourable mention for their algebraical solutions being the only two who have perceived that the question leads to an indeterminate equation. E. W. brings a charge of untruthfulness against the aged knight—a serious charge, for he was the very pink of chivalry! She says "According to the data given, the time at the summit affords no clue to the total distance. It does not enable us to state precisely to an inch how much level and how much hill there was on the road." "Fair damsel," the aged knight replies, "—if, as I surmise, thy initials denote Early Womanhood—bethink thee that the word 'enable' is thine, not mine. I did but ask the time of reaching the hill-top as my condition for further parley. If now thou wilt not grant that I am a truth-loving man, then will I affirm that those same initials denote Envenomed Wickedness!"

CLASS LIST

I

A Marlborough Boy.
Putney Walker.

II

Blithe.
E. W.
L. B.
O. V. L.
Rose.
Sea Breeze.
{Simple Susan.
{Money-Spinner.

Blithe has made so ingenious an addition to the problem, and Simple Susan and Co. have solved it in such tuneful verse, that I record both their answers in full. I have altered a word or two in Blithe's—which I trust she will excuse; it did not seem quite clear as it stood.

"Yet stay," said the youth, as a gleam of inspiration lighted up the relaxing muscles of his quiescent features. "Stay. Methinks it matters little when we reached that summit, the crown of our toil. For in the space of time wherein we clambered up one mile and bounded down the same on our return, we could have trudged the twain on the level. We have plodded, then, four-and-twenty miles in these six mortal hours; for never a moment did we stop for catching of fleeting breath or for gazing on the scene around!"

"Very good," said the old man. "Twelve miles out and twelve miles in. And we reached the top some time between six and seven of the clock. Now mark me! For every five minutes that had fled since six of the clock when we stood on yonder peak, so many miles had we toiled upwards on the dreary mountainside!"

The youth moaned and rushed into the hostel.

Blithe.

The elder and the younger knight,
They sallied forth at three;
How far they went on level ground
It matters not to me;
What time they reached the foot of hill,
When they began to mount,
Are problems which I hold to be
Of very small account.

The moment that each waved his hat
Upon the topmost peak—
To trivial query such as this
No answer will I seek.
Yet can I tell the distance well
They must have travelled o'er:
On hill and plain, 'twixt three and nine,
The miles were twenty-four.

Four miles an hour their steady pace
Along the level track,
Three when they climbed—but six when they
Came swiftly striding back
Adown the hill; and little skill
It needs, methinks, to show,
Up hill and down together told,
Four miles an hour they go.

For whether long or short the time
Upon the hill they spent,
Two thirds were passed in going up,
One third in the descent.
Two thirds at three, one third at six,
If rightly reckoned o'er,
Will make one whole at four—the tale
Is tangled now no more.

Simple Susan
Money Spinner

ANSWERS TO KNOT II

§ 1. The Dinner Party

Problem. — "The Governor of Kgovjni wants to give a very small dinner party, and invites his father's brother-in-law, his brother's father-in-law, his father-in-law's brother, and his brother-in-law's father. Find the number of guests."

Answer. — "One."

In this genealogy, males are denoted by capitals, and females by small letters.

The Governor is E and his guest is C.

Ten answers have been received. Of these, one is wrong, Galanthus Nivalis Major, who insists on inviting two guests, one being the Governor's wife's brother's father. If she had taken his sister's husband's father instead, she would have found it possible to reduce the guests to one.

Of the nine who send right answers, Sea-Breeze is the very faintest breath that ever bore the name! She simply states that the Governor's uncle might fulfill all the conditions "by intermarriages"! "Wind of the western sea," you have had a very narrow escape! Be thankful to appear in the Class-list at all! Bog-Oak and Bradshaw of the Future use genealogies which require 16 people instead of 14, by inviting the Governor's father's sister's husband instead of his father's wife's brother. I cannot think this so good a solution as one that requires only 14. Caius and Valentine deserve special mention as the only two who have supplied genealogies.

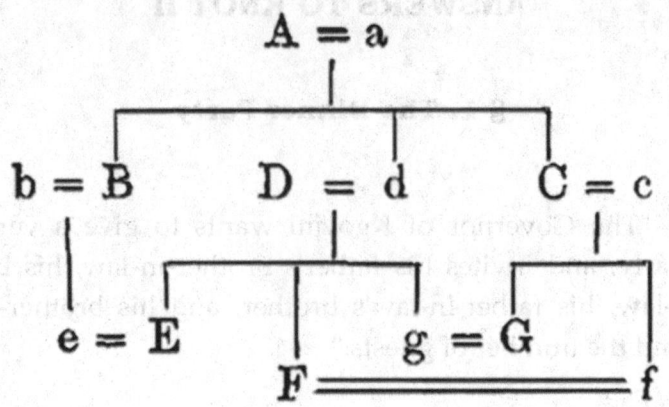

CLASS LIST

I

Bee.
Caius.
M. M.
Matthew Matticks.
Old Cat.
Valentine.

II

Bog-Oak.
Bradshaw of the Future.

III

Sea-Breeze.

§ 2. The Lodgings

Problem.—"A Square has 20 doors on each side, which contains 21 equal parts. They are numbered all round, beginning at one corner. From which of the four, Nos. 9, 25, 52, 73, is the sum of the distances, to the other three, least?"

Answer.—"From No. 9."

Let A be No. 9, B No. 25, C No. 52, and D No. 73.

> Then AB = $\sqrt{(12^2 + 5^2)} = \sqrt{169} = 13$;
> AC = 21;
> AD = $\sqrt{(9^2 + 8^2)} = \sqrt{145} = 12+$
> (N.B. i.e. "between 12 and 13.")
> BC = $\sqrt{(16^2 + 12^2)} = \sqrt{400} = 20$;
> BD = $\sqrt{(3^2 + 21^2)} = \sqrt{450} = 21+$;
> CD = $\sqrt{(9^2 + 13^2)} = \sqrt{250} = 15+$;

Hence sum of distances from A is between 46 and 47; from B, between 54 and 55; from C, between 56 and 57; from D, between 48 and 51. (Why not "between 48 and 49"? Make this out for yourselves.) Hence the sum is least for A.

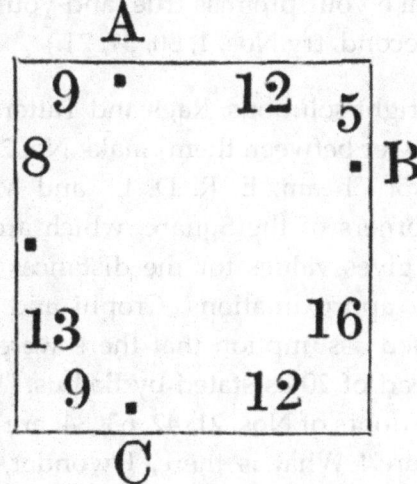

Twenty-five solutions have been received. Of these, 15 must be marked "0," 5 are partly right, and 5 right. Of the 15, I may dismiss Alphabetical Phantom, Bog-Oak, Dinah Mite, Fifee, Galanthus Nivalis Major (I fear the cold spring has blighted our Snowdrop), Guy, H.M.S. Pinafore, Janet, and Valentine with the simple remark that they insist on the unfortunate lodgers keeping to the pavement. (I used the words "crossed to Number Seventy-three" for the special purpose of showing that short cuts were possible.) Sea-Breeze does the same, and adds that "the result would be the same" even if they crossed the Square, but gives no proof of this. M. M. draws a diagram, and says that No. 9 is the house, "as the diagram shows." I cannot see how it does so. Old Cat assumes that the house must be No. 9 or No. 73. She does not explain how she estimates the distances. BEE's Arithmetic is faulty: she makes $\sqrt{169} + \sqrt{442} + \sqrt{130} =$ 741. (I suppose you mean $\sqrt{741}$, which would be a little nearer the truth. But roots cannot be added in this manner. Do you think $\sqrt{9} + \sqrt{16}$ is 25, or even $\sqrt{25}$?) But Ayr's state is more perilous still: she draws illogical conclusions with a frightful calmness. After pointing out (rightly) that AC is less than BD she says, "therefore the nearest house to the other three must be A or C." And again, after pointing out (rightly) that B and D are both within the half-square containing A, she says "therefore" AB + AD must be less than BC + CD. (There is no logical force in either "therefore." For the first, try Nos. 1, 21, 60, 70: this will make your premiss true, and your conclusion false. Similarly, for the second, try Nos. 1, 30, 51, 71.)

Of the five partly-right solutions, Rags and Tatters and Mad Hatter (who send one answer between them) make No. 25 6 units from the corner instead of 5. Cheam, E. R. D. L., and Meggy Potts leave openings at the corners of the Square, which are not in the data: moreover Cheam gives values for the distances without any hint that they are only approximations. Crophi and Mophi make the bold and unfounded assumption that there were really 21 houses on each side, instead of 20 as stated by Balbus. "We may assume," they add, "that the doors of Nos. 21, 42, 63, 84, are invisible from the centre of the Square"! What is there, I wonder, that Crophi and Mophi would not assume?

Of the five who are wholly right, I think Bradshaw Of the Future, Caius, Clifton C., and Martreb deserve special praise for their full analytical solutions. Matthew Matticks picks out No. 9, and proves it to be the right house in two ways, very neatly and ingeniously, but why he picks it out does not appear. It is an excellent synthetical proof, but lacks the analysis which the other four supply.

CLASS LIST

I

Bradshaw of the Future
Caius.
Clifton C.
Martreb.

II

Matthew Matticks.

III

Cheam.
Crophi and Mophi.
E. R. D. L.
Meggy Potts.
{Rags and Tatters.
{Mad Hatter.

A remonstrance has reached me from Scrutator on the subject of Knot I., which he declares was "no problem at all." "Two questions," he says, "are put. To solve one there is no data: the other answers itself." As to the first point, Scrutator is mistaken; there are (not "is") data sufficient to answer the question. As to the other, it is

55

interesting to know that the question "answers itself," and I am sure it does the question great credit: still I fear I cannot enter it on the list of winners, as this competition is only open to human beings.

ANSWERS TO KNOT III

Problem.—(1) "Two travellers, starting at the same time, went opposite ways round a circular railway. Trains start each way every 15 minutes, the easterly ones going round in 3 hours, the westerly in 2. How many trains did each meet on the way, not counting trains met at the terminus itself?" (2) "They went round, as before, each traveller counting as 'one' the train containing the other traveller. How many did each meet?"

Answers.—(1) 19. (2) The easterly traveller met 12; the other 8.

The trains one way took 180 minutes, the other way 120. Let us take the L. C. M., 360, and divide the railway into 360 units. Then one set of trains went at the rate of 2 units a minute and at intervals of 30 units; the other at the rate of 3 units a minute and at intervals of 45 units. An easterly train starting has 45 units between it and the first train it will meet: it does 2-5ths of this while the other does 3-5ths, and thus meets it at the end of 18 units, and so all the way round. A westerly train starting has 30 units between it and the first train it will meet: it does 3-5ths of this while the other does 2-5ths, and thus meets it at the end of 18 units, and so all the way round. Hence if the railway be divided, by 19 posts, into 20 parts, each containing 18 units, trains meet at every post, and, in (1), each traveller passes 19 posts in going round, and so meets 19 trains. But, in (2), the easterly traveller only begins to count after traversing 2-5ths of the journey, i.e., on reaching the 8th post, and so counts 12 posts: similarly the other counts 8. They meet at the end of 2-5ths of 3 hours, or 3-5ths of 2 hours, i.e., 72 minutes.

Forty-five answers have been received. Of these 12 are beyond the reach of discussion, as they give no working. I can but enumerate their names. Ardmore, E. A., F. A. D., L. D., Matthew Matticks, M. E. T., Poo-Poo, and The Red Queen are all wrong. Beta and Rowena have got (1) right and (2) wrong. Cheeky Bob and Nairam give the right answers, but it may perhaps make the one less cheeky, and

57

induce the other to take a less inverted view of things, to be informed that, if this had been a competition for a prize, they would have got no marks. [N.B.—I have not ventured to put E. A.'s name in full, as she only gave it provisionally, in case her answer should prove right.]

Of the 33 answers for which the working is given, 10 are wrong; 11 half-wrong and half-right; 3 right, except that they cherish the delusion that it was Clara who travelled in the easterly train—a point which the data do not enable us to settle; and 9 wholly right.

The 10 wrong answers are from Bo-Peep, Financier, I. W. T., Kate B., M. A. H., Q. Y. Z., Sea-Gull, Thistledown, Tom-Quad, and an unsigned one. Bo-Peep rightly says that the easterly traveller met all trains which started during the 3 hours of her trip, as well as all which started during the previous 2 hours, i.e., all which started at the commencements of 20 periods of 15 minutes each; and she is right in striking out the one she met at the moment of starting; but wrong in striking out the last train, for she did not meet this at the terminus, but 15 minutes before she got there. She makes the same mistake in (2). Financier thinks that any train, met for the second time, is not to be counted. I. W. T. finds, by a process which is not stated, that the travellers met at the end of 71 minutes and 26½ seconds. Kate B. thinks the trains which are met on starting and on arriving are never to be counted, even when met elsewhere. Q. Y. Z. tries a rather complex algebraical solution, and succeeds in finding the time of meeting correctly: all else is wrong. Sea-Gull seems to think that, in (1), the easterly train stood still for 3 hours; and says that, in (2), the travellers met at the end of 71 minutes 40 seconds. Thistledown nobly confesses to having tried no calculation, but merely having drawn a picture of the railway and counted the trains; in (1), she counts wrong; in (2) she makes them meet in 75 minutes. Tom-Quad omits (1): in (2) he makes Clara count the train she met on her arrival. The unsigned one is also unintelligible; it states that the travellers go "1-24th more than the total distance to be traversed"! The "Clara" theory, already referred to, is adopted by

5 of these, viz., Bo-Peep, Financier, Kate B., Tom-Quad, and the nameless writer.

The 11 half-right answers are from Bog-Oak, Bridget, Castor, Cheshire Cat, G. E. B., Guy, Mary, M. A. H., Old Maid, R. W., and Vendredi. All these adopt the "Clara" theory. Castor omits (1). Vendredi gets (1) right, but in (2) makes the same mistake as Bo-Peep. I notice in your solution a marvellous proportion-sum:—"300 miles: 2 hours :: one mile: 24 seconds." May I venture to advise your acquiring, as soon as possible, an utter disbelief in the possibility of a ratio existing between miles and hours? Do not be disheartened by your two friends' sarcastic remarks on your "roundabout ways." Their short method, of adding 12 and 8, has the slight disadvantage of bringing the answer wrong: even a "roundabout" method is better than that! M. A. H., in (2), makes the travellers count "one" after they met, not when they met. Cheshire Cat and Old Maid get "20" as answer for (1), by forgetting to strike out the train met on arrival. The others all get "18" in various ways. Bog-Oak, Guy, and R. W. divide the trains which the westerly traveller has to meet into 2 sets, viz., those already on the line, which they (rightly) make "11," and those which started during her 2 hours' journey (exclusive of train met on arrival), which they (wrongly) make "7"; and they make a similar mistake with the easterly train. Bridget (rightly) says that the westerly traveller met a train every 6 minutes for 2 hours, but (wrongly) makes the number "20"; it should be "21." G. E. B. adopts Bo-Peep's method, but (wrongly) strikes out (for the easterly traveller) the train which started at the commencement of the previous 2 hours. Mary thinks a train, met on arrival, must not be counted, even when met on a previous occasion.

The 3, who are wholly right but for the unfortunate "Clara" theory, are F. Lee, G. S. C., and X. A. B.

And now "descend, ye classic Ten!" who have solved the whole problem. Your names are Aix-les-Bains, Algernon Bray (thanks for a friendly remark, which comes with a heart-warmth that not even the Atlantic could chill), Arvon, Bradshaw of the Future, Fifee, H. L.

R., J. L. O., Omega, S. S. G., and Waiting for the Train. Several of these have put Clara, provisionally, into the easterly train: but they seem to have understood that the data do not decide that point.

CLASS LIST

I

Aix-les-Bains.
Algernon Bray.
Bradshaw of the Future.
Fifee.
H. L. R.
Omega.
S. S. G.
Waiting for the train.

II

Arvon.
J. L. O.

III

F. Lee.
G. S. C.
X. A. B.

Problem.—"There are 5 sacks, of which Nos. 1, 2, weigh 12 lbs.; Nos. 2, 3, 13½ lbs.; Nos. 3, 4, 11½ lbs.; Nos. 4, 5, 8 lbs.; Nos. 1, 3, 5, 16 lbs. Required the weight of each sack."

Answer.—"5½, 6½, 7, 4½, 3½."

The sum of all the weighings, 61 lbs., includes sack No. 3 thrice and each other twice. Deducting twice the sum of the 1st and 4th weighings, we get 21 lbs. for thrice No. 3, i.e., 7 lbs. for No. 3. Hence, the 2nd and 3rd weighings give 6½ lbs., 4½ lbs. for Nos. 2, 4; and hence again, the 1st and 4th weighings give 5½ lbs., 3½ lbs., for Nos. 1, 5.

Ninety-seven answers have been received. Of these, 15 are beyond the reach of discussion, as they give no working. I can but enumerate their names, and I take this opportunity of saying that this is the last time I shall put on record the names of competitors who give no sort of clue to the process by which their answers were obtained. In guessing a conundrum, or in catching a flea, we do not expect the breathless victor to give us afterwards, in cold blood, a history of the mental or muscular efforts by which he achieved success; but a mathematical calculation is another thing. The names of this "mute inglorious" band are Common Sense, D. E. R., Douglas, E. L., Ellen, I. M. T., J. M. C., Joseph, Knot I, Lucy, Meek, M. F. C., Pyramus, Shah, Veritas.

Of the eighty-two answers with which the working, or some approach to it, is supplied, one is wrong: seventeen have given solutions which are (from one cause or another) practically valueless: the remaining sixty-four I shall try to arrange in a Class-list, according to the varying degrees of shortness and neatness to which they seem to have attained.

The solitary wrong answer is from Nell. To be thus "alone in the crowd" is a distinction—a painful one, no doubt, but still a distinction. I am sorry for you, my dear young lady, and I seem to hear your tearful exclamation, when you read these lines, "Ah! This is the knell of all my hopes!" Why, oh why, did you assume that the 4th and 5th bags weighed 4 lbs. each? And why did you not test your answers? However, please try again: and please don't change your nom-de-plume: let us have Nell in the First Class next time!

The seventeen whose solutions are practically valueless are Ardmore, A ready Reckoner, Arthur, Bog-Lark, Bog-Oak, Bridget, First Attempt, J. L. C., M. E. T., Rose, Rowena, Sea-Breeze, Sylvia, Thistledown, Three-Fifths Asleep, Vendredi, and Winifred. Bog-Lark tries it by a sort of "rule of false," assuming experimentally that Nos. 1, 2, weigh 6 lbs. each, and having thus produced 17½, instead of 16, as the weight of 1, 3, and 5, she removes "the superfluous pound and a half," but does not explain how she knows from which to take it. Three-fifths Asleep says that (when in that peculiar state) "it seemed perfectly clear" to her that, "3 out of the 5 sacks being weighed twice over, 2/5 of 45 = 27, must be the total weight of the 5 sacks." As to which I can only say, with the Captain, "it beats me entirely!" Winifred, on the plea that "one must have a starting-point," assumes (what I fear is a mere guess) that No. 1 weighed 5½ lbs. The rest all do it, wholly or partly, by guess-work.

The problem is of course (as any Algebraist sees at once) a case of "simultaneous simple equations." It is, however, easily soluble by Arithmetic only; and, when this is the case, I hold that it is bad workmanship to use the more complex method. I have not, this time, given more credit to arithmetical solutions; but in future problems I shall (other things being equal) give the highest marks to those who use the simplest machinery. I have put into Class I. those whose answers seemed specially short and neat, and into Class III. those that seemed specially long or clumsy. Of this last set, A. C. M., Furze-Bush, James, Partridge, R. W., and Waiting for the Train, have sent long wandering solutions, the substitutions having no definite method, but seeming to have been made to see what would come of it. Chilpome and Dublin Boy omit some of the working. Arvon Marlborough Boy only finds the weight of one sack.

CLASS LIST

I

B. E. D.
C. H.
Constance Johnson.
Greystead.
Guy.
Hoopoe.
J. F. A.
M. A. H.
Number Five.
Pedro.
R. E. X.
Seven Old Men.
Vis Inertiæ.
Willy B.
Yahoo.

II

American Subscriber.
An appreciative schoolma'am.
Ayr.
Bradshaw of the Future.
Cheam.
C. M. G.
Dinah Mite.
Duckwing.
E. C. M.

E. N. Lowry.
Era.
Euroclydon.
F. H. W.
Fifee.
G. E. B.
Harlequin.
Hawthorn.
Hough Green.
J. A. B.
Jack Tar.
J. B. B.
Kgovjni.
Land Lubber.
L. D.
Magpie.
Mary.
Mhruxi.
Minnie.
Money-Spinner.
Nairam.
Old Cat.
Polichinelle.
Simple Susan.
S. S. G.
Thisbe.
Verena.
Wamba.
Wolfe.
Wykehamicus.
Y. M. A. H.

III

A. C. M.
Arvon Marlborough Boy.
Chilpome.

Dublin Boy.
Furze-Bush.
James.
Partridge.
R. W.
Waiting for the Train.

Problem.—To mark pictures, giving 3 x's to 2 or 3, 2 to 4 or 5, and 1 to 9 or 10; also giving 3 o's to 1 or 2, 2 to 3 or 4 and 1 to 8 or 9; so as to mark the smallest possible number of pictures, and to give them the largest possible number of marks.

Answer.—10 pictures; 29 marks; arranged thus:—

```
x x x x x x x x x o
x x x x x     o o o o
x x o o o o o o o o
```

Solution.—By giving all the x's possible, putting into brackets the optional ones, we get 10 pictures marked thus:—

```
x x x x x x x x x (x)
x x x x (x)
x x (x)
```

By then assigning o's in the same way, beginning at the other end, we get 9 pictures marked thus:—

```
                    (o) o

              (o) o o o

        (o) o o o o o o o
```

All we have now to do is to run these two wedges as close together as they will go, so as to get the minimum number of pictures—— erasing optional marks where by so doing we can run them closer, but otherwise letting them stand. There are 10 necessary marks in the 1st row, and in the 3rd; but only 7 in the 2nd. Hence we erase all optional marks in the 1st and 3rd rows, but let them stand in the 2nd.

Twenty-two answers have been received. Of these 11 give no

working; so, in accordance with what I announced in my last review of answers, I leave them unnamed, merely mentioning that 5 are right and 6 wrong.

Of the eleven answers with which some working is supplied, 3 are wrong. C. H. begins with the rash assertion that under the given conditions "the sum is impossible. For," he or she adds (these initialed correspondents are dismally vague beings to deal with: perhaps "it" would be a better pronoun), "10 is the least possible number of pictures" (granted): "therefore we must either give 2 x's to 6, or 2 o's to 5." Why "must," oh alphabetical phantom? It is nowhere ordained that every picture "must" have 3 marks! Fifee sends a folio page of solution, which deserved a better fate: she offers 3 answers, in each of which 10 pictures are marked, with 30 marks; in one she gives 2 x's to 6 pictures; in another to 7; in the 3rd she gives 2 o's to 5; thus in every case ignoring the conditions. (I pause to remark that the condition "2 x's to 4 or 5 pictures" can only mean "either to 4 or else to 5": if, as one competitor holds, it might mean any number not less than 4, the words "or 5" would be superfluous.) I. E. A. (I am happy to say that none of these bloodless phantoms appear this time in the class-list. Is it IDEA with the "D" left out?) gives 2 x's to 6 pictures. She then takes me to task for using the word "ought" instead of "nought." No doubt, to one who thus rebels against the rules laid down for her guidance, the word must be distasteful. But does not I. E. A. remember the parallel case of "adder"? That creature was originally "a nadder": then the two words took to bandying the poor "n" backwards and forwards like a shuttlecock, the final state of the game being "an adder." May not "a nought" have similarly become "an ought"? Anyhow, "oughts and crosses" is a very old game. I don't think I ever heard it called "noughts and crosses."

In the following Class-list, I hope the solitary occupant of III. will sheathe her claws when she hears how narrow an escape she has had of not being named at all. Her account of the process by which she got the answer is so meagre that, like the nursery tale of "Jack-a-

67

Minory" (I trust I. E. A. will be merciful to the spelling), it is scarcely to be distinguished from "zero."

CLASS LIST

I

Guy.
Old Cat.
Sea-Breeze.

II

Ayr.
Bradshaw of the Future.
F. Lee.
H. Vernon.

III

Cat.

Problem 1.—A and B began the year with only 1,000l. a-piece. They borrowed nought; they stole nought. On the next New-Year's Day they had 60,000l. between them. How did they do it?

Solution.—They went that day to the Bank of England. A stood in front of it, while B went round and stood behind it.

Two answers have been received, both worthy of much honour. Addlepate makes them borrow "0" and steal "0," and uses both cyphers by putting them at the right-hand end of the 1,000l., thus producing 100,000l., which is well over the mark. But (or to express it in Latin) At Spes infracta has solved it even more ingeniously: with the first cypher she turns the "1" of the 1,000l. into a "9," and adds the result to the original sum, thus getting 10,000l.: and in this, by means of the other "0," she turns the "1" into a "6," thus hitting the exact 60,000l.

CLASS LIST

I

At Spes Infracta.

II

Addlepate.

Problem 2.—L makes 5 scarves, while M makes 2: Z makes 4 while L makes 3. Five scarves of Z's weigh one of L's; 5 of M's weigh 3 of Z's. One of M's is as warm as 4 of Z's: and one of L's as warm as 3 of

M's. Which is best, giving equal weight in the result to rapidity of work, lightness, and warmth?

Answer.—The order is M, L, Z.

Solution.—As to rapidity (other things being constant) L's merit is to M's in the ratio of 5 to 2: Z's to L's in the ratio of 4 to 3. In order to get one set of 3 numbers fulfilling these conditions, it is perhaps simplest to take the one that occurs twice as unity, and reduce the others to fractions: this gives, for L, M, and Z, the marks 1, 2/5, 2/3. In estimating for lightness, we observe that the greater the weight, the less the merit, so that Z's merit is to L's as 5 to 1. Thus the marks for lightness are 1/5, 2/3, 1. And similarly, the marks for warmth are 3, 1, 1/4. To get the total result, we must multiply L's 3 marks together, and do the same for M and for Z. The final numbers are 1 × 1/5 × 3, 2/5 × 2/3 × 1, 2/3 × 1 × 1/4; i.e. 3/5, 2/3, 1/3; i.e. multiplying throughout by 15 (which will not alter the proportion), 9, 10, 5; showing the order of merit to be M, L, Z.

Twenty-nine answers have been received, of which five are right, and twenty-four wrong. These hapless ones have all (with three exceptions) fallen into the error of adding the proportional numbers together, for each candidate, instead of multiplying. Why the latter is right, rather than the former, is fully proved in text-books, so I will not occupy space by stating it here: but it can be illustrated very easily by the case of length, breadth, and depth. Suppose A and B are rival diggers of rectangular tanks: the amount of work done is evidently measured by the number of cubical feet dug out. Let A dig a tank 10 feet long, 10 wide, 2 deep: let B dig one 6 feet long, 5 wide, 10 deep. The cubical contents are 200, 300; i.e. B is best digger in the ratio of 3 to 2. Now try marking for length, width, and depth, separately; giving a maximum mark of 10 to the best in each contest, and then adding the results!

Of the twenty-four malefactors, one gives no working, and so has no real claim to be named; but I break the rule for once, in deference to its success in Problem 1: he, she, or it, is Addlepate. The other twenty-three may be divided into five groups.

First and worst are, I take it, those who put the rightful winner last; arranging them as "Lolo, Zuzu, Mimi." The names of these desperate wrong-doers are Ayr, Bradshaw of the Future, Furzebush and Pollux (who send a joint answer), Greystead, Guy, Old Hen, and Simple Susan. The latter was once best of all; the Old Hen has taken advantage of her simplicity, and beguiled her with the chaff which was the bane of her own chickenhood.

Secondly, I point the finger of scorn at those who have put the worst candidate at the top; arranging them as "Zuzu, Mimi, Lolo." They are Graecia, M. M., Old Cat, and R. E. X. "'Tis Greece, but—."

The third set have avoided both these enormities, and have even succeeded in putting the worst last, their answer being "Lolo, Mimi, Zuzu." Their names are Ayr (who also appears among the "quite too too"), Clifton C., F. B., Fifee, Grig, Janet, and Mrs. Sairey Gamp. F. B. has not fallen into the common error; she multiplies together the proportionate numbers she gets, but in getting them she goes wrong, by reckoning warmth as a de-merit. Possibly she is "Freshly Burnt," or comes "From Bombay." Janet and Mrs. Sairey Gamp have also avoided this error: the method they have adopted is shrouded in mystery—I scarcely feel competent to criticize it. Mrs. Gamp says "if Zuzu makes 4 while Lolo makes 3, Zuzu makes 6 while Lolo makes 5 (bad reasoning), while Mimi makes 2." From this she concludes "therefore Zuzu excels in speed by 1" (i.e. when compared with Lolo; but what about Mimi?). She then compares the 3 kinds of excellence, measured on this mystic scale. Janet takes the statement, that "Lolo makes 5 while Mimi makes 2," to prove that "Lolo makes 3 while Mimi makes 1 and Zuzu 4" (worse reasoning than Mrs. Gamp's), and thence concludes that "Zuzu excels in speed by 1/8"! Janet should have been Adeline, "mystery of mysteries!"

The fourth set actually put Mimi at the top, arranging them as "Mimi, Zuzu, Lolo." They are Marquis and Co., Martreb, S. B. B. (first initial scarcely legible: may be meant for "J"), and Stanza.

The fifth set consist of An ancient Fish and Camel. These ill-assorted comrades, by dint of foot and fin, have scrambled into the right answer, but, as their method is wrong, of course it counts for nothing. Also An ancient Fish has very ancient and fishlike ideas as to how numbers represent merit: she says "Lolo gains 2½ on Mimi." Two and a half what? Fish, fish, art thou in thy duty?

Of the five winners I put Balbus and The elder Traveller slightly below the other three—Balbus for defective reasoning, the other for scanty working. Balbus gives two reasons for saying that addition of marks is not the right method, and then adds "it follows that the decision must be made by multiplying the marks together." This is hardly more logical than to say "This is not Spring: therefore it must be Autumn."

CLASS LIST

I

Dinah Mite.
E. B. D. L.
Joram.

II

Balbus.
The Elder Traveller.

With regard to Knot V., I beg to express to Vis Inertiæ and to any others who, like her, understood the condition to be that every marked picture must have three marks, my sincere regret that the unfortunate phrase "fill the columns with oughts and crosses" should have caused them to waste so much time and trouble. I can only repeat that a literal interpretation of "fill" would seem to me to require that every picture in the gallery should be marked. Vis Inertiæ would have been in the First Class if she had sent in the solution she now offers.

Problem.—Given that one glass of lemonade, 3 sandwiches, and 7 biscuits, cost 1s. 2d.; and that one glass of lemonade, 4 sandwiches, and 10 biscuits, cost 1s. 5d.: find the cost of (1) a glass of lemonade, a sandwich, and a biscuit; and (2) 2 glasses of lemonade, 3 sandwiches, and 5 biscuits.

Answer.—(1) 8d.; (2) 1s. 7d.

Solution.—This is best treated algebraically. Let x = the cost (in pence) of a glass of lemonade, y of a sandwich, and z of a biscuit. Then we have $x + 3y + 7z = 14$, and $x + 4y + 10z = 17$. And we require the values of $x + y + z$, and of $2x + 3y + 5z$. Now, from two equations only, we cannot find, separately, the values of three unknowns: certain combinations of them may, however, be found. Also we know that we can, by the help of the given equations, eliminate 2 of the 3 unknowns from the quantity whose value is required, which will then contain one only. If, then, the required value is ascertainable at all, it can only be by the 3rd unknown vanishing of itself: otherwise the problem is impossible.

Let us then eliminate lemonade and sandwiches, and reduce everything to biscuits—a state of things even more depressing than "if all the world were apple-pie"—by subtracting the 1st equation from the 2nd, which eliminates lemonade, and gives $y + 3z = 3$, or $y = 3-3z$; and then substituting this value of y in the 1st, which gives $x-2z = 5$, i.e. $x = 5 + 2z$. Now if we substitute these values of x, y, in the quantities whose values are required, the first becomes $(5 + 2z) + (3-3z) + z$, i.e. 8: and the second becomes $2(5 + 2z) + 3(3-3z) + 5z$, i.e. 19. Hence the answers are (1) 8d., (2) 1s. 7d.

The above is a universal method: that is, it is absolutely certain either to produce the answer, or to prove that no answer is possible. The question may also be solved by combining the quantities whose values are given, so as to form those whose values are required.

This is merely a matter of ingenuity and good luck: and as it may fail, even when the thing is possible, and is of no use in proving it impossible, I cannot rank this method as equal in value with the other. Even when it succeeds, it may prove a very tedious process. Suppose the 26 competitors, who have sent in what I may call accidental solutions, had had a question to deal with where every number contained 8 or 10 digits! I suspect it would have been a case of "silvered is the raven hair" (see "Patience") before any solution would have been hit on by the most ingenious of them.

Forty-five answers have come in, of which 44 give, I am happy to say, some sort of working, and therefore deserve to be mentioned by name, and to have their virtues, or vices as the case may be, discussed. Thirteen have made assumptions to which they have no right, and so cannot figure in the Class-list, even though, in 10 of the 13 cases, the answer is right. Of the remaining 28, no less than 26 have sent in accidental solutions, and therefore fall short of the highest honours.

I will now discuss individual cases, taking the worst first, as my custom is.

Froggy gives no working—at least this is all he gives: after stating the given equations, he says "therefore the difference, 1 sandwich + 3 biscuits, = 3d.": then follow the amounts of the unknown bills, with no further hint as to how he got them. Froggy has had a very narrow escape of not being named at all!

Of those who are wrong, Vis Inertiæ has sent in a piece of incorrect working. Peruse the horrid details, and shudder! She takes x (call it "y") as the cost of a sandwich, and concludes (rightly enough) that a biscuit will cost (3-y)/3. She then subtracts the second equation from the first, and deduces 3y + 7 × (3-y)/3-4y + 10 × (3-y)/3 = 3. By making two mistakes in this line, she brings out y = 2⁄2. Try it again, oh Vis Inertiæ! Away with Inertiæ: infuse a little more Vis: and you will bring out the correct (though uninteresting) result, 0 = 0! This will show you that it is hopeless to try to coax any one of these 3 unknowns to reveal its separate value. The other competitor, who is wrong throughout, is either J. M. C. or T. M. C.: but, whether he be a Juvenile Mis-Calculator or a True Mathematician Confused, he makes the answers 7d. and 1s. 5d. He assumes, with Too Much Confidence, that biscuits were ½d. each, and that Clara paid for 8, though she only ate 7!

We will now consider the 13 whose working is wrong, though the answer is right: and, not to measure their demerits too exactly, I will take them in alphabetical order. Anita finds (rightly) that "1 sandwich and 3 biscuits cost 3d.," and proceeds "therefore 1 sandwich = 1½d., 3 biscuits = 1½d., 1 lemonade = 6d." Dinah Mite begins like Anita: and thence proves (rightly) that a biscuit costs less than a 1d.: whence she concludes (wrongly) that it must cost ½d. F. C. W. is so beautifully resigned to the certainty of a verdict of "guilty," that I have hardly the heart to utter the word, without adding a "recommended to mercy owing to extenuating circumstances." But really, you know, where are the extenuating circumstances? She begins by assuming that lemonade is 4d. a glass, and sandwiches 3d. each, (making with the 2 given equations, four conditions to be fulfilled by three miserable unknowns!). And, having (naturally) developed this into a contradiction, she then tries 5d. and 2d. with a similar result. (N.B. This process might have been carried on through the whole of the Tertiary Period, without gratifying one single Megatherium.) She then, by a "happy thought," tries half-penny biscuits, and so obtains a consistent result. This may be a good solution, viewing the problem as a conundrum: but it is not scientific. Janet identifies sandwiches with biscuits! "One sandwich + 3 biscuits" she makes equal to "4." Four what? Mayfair makes the astounding assertion that the equation, $s + 3b = 3$, "is evidently only satisfied by $s = 2/2$, $b = ½$"! Old Cat believes that the assumption that a sandwich costs 1½d. is "the only way to avoid unmanageable fractions." But why avoid them? Is there not a certain glow of triumph in taming such a fraction? "Ladies and gentlemen, the fraction now before you is one that for years defied all efforts of a refining nature: it was, in a word, hopelessly vulgar.

Treating it as a circulating decimal (the treadmill of fractions) only made matters worse. As a last resource, I reduced it to its lowest terms, and extracted its square root!" Joking apart, let me thank Old Cat for some very kind words of sympathy, in reference to a correspondent (whose name I am happy to say I have now forgotten) who had found fault with me as a discourteous critic. O. V. L. is beyond my comprehension. He takes the given equations as (1) and (2): thence, by the process [(2)-(1)] deduces (rightly) equation (3) viz. s + 3b = 3: and thence again, by the process [×3 (a hopeless mystery), deduces 3s + 4b = 4. I have nothing to say about it: I give it up. Sea-Breeze says "it is immaterial to the answer" (why?) "in what proportion 3d. is divided between the sandwich and the 3 biscuits": so she assumes s = 1½d., b = ½d. Stanza is one of a very irregular metre. At first she (like Janet) identifies sandwiches with biscuits. She then tries two assumptions (s = 1, b = 2⁄3, and s = ½ b = 2⁄6), and (naturally) ends in contradictions. Then she returns to the first assumption, and finds the 3 unknowns separately: quod est absurdum. Stiletto identifies sandwiches and biscuits, as "articles." Is the word ever used by confectioners? I fancied "What is the next article, Ma'am?" was limited to linendrapers. Two Sisters first assume that biscuits are 4 a penny, and then that they are 2 a penny, adding that "the answer will of course be the same in both cases." It is a dreamy remark, making one feel something like Macbeth grasping at the spectral dagger. "Is this a statement that I see before me?" If you were to say "we both walked the same way this morning," and I were to say "one of you walked the same way, but the other didn't," which of the three would be the most hopelessly confused? Turtle Pyate (what is a Turtle Pyate, please?) and Old Crow, who send a joint answer, and Y. Y., adopt the same method. Y. Y. gets the equation s + 3b = 3: and then says "this sum must be apportioned in one of the three following ways." It may be, I grant you: but Y. Y. do you say "must"? I fear it is possible for Y. Y. to be two Y's. The other two conspirators are less positive: they say it "can" be so divided: but they add "either of the three prices being right"! This is bad grammar and bad arithmetic at once, oh mysterious birds!

Of those who win honours, The Shetland Snark must have the 3rd class all to himself. He has only answered half the question, viz. the amount of Clara's luncheon: the two little old ladies he pitilessly leaves in the midst of their "difficulty." I beg to assure him (with thanks for his friendly remarks) that entrance-fees and subscriptions are things unknown in that most economical of clubs, "The Knot-Untiers."

The authors of the 26 "accidental" solutions differ only in the number of steps they have taken between the data and the answers. In order to do them full justice I have arranged the 2nd class in sections, according to the number of steps. The two Kings are fearfully deliberate! I suppose walking quick, or taking short cuts, is inconsistent with kingly dignity: but really, in reading Theseus' solution, one almost fancied he was "marking time," and making no advance at all! The other King will, I hope, pardon me for having altered "Coal" into "Cole." King Coilus, or Coil, seems to have reigned soon after Arthur's time. Henry of Huntingdon identifies him with the King Coël who first built walls round Colchester, which was named after him. In the Chronicle of Robert of Gloucester we read:—

"Aftur Kyng Aruirag, of wam we habbeth y told,
Marius ys sone was kyng, quoynte mon & bold.
And ys sone was aftur hym, Coil was ys name,
Bothe it were quoynte men, & of noble fame."

Balbus lays it down as a general principle that "in order to ascertain the cost of any one luncheon, it must come to the same amount upon two different assumptions." (Query. Should not "it" be "we"? Otherwise the luncheon is represented as wishing to ascertain its own cost!) He then makes two assumptions—one, that sandwiches cost nothing; the other, that biscuits cost nothing, (either arrangement would lead to the shop being inconveniently crowded!)—and brings out the unknown luncheons as 8d. and 19d., on each assumption. He then concludes that this agreement of results "shows that the answers are correct." Now I propose to disprove his general law by simply giving one instance of its failing. One instance is quite enough. In logical language, in order to disprove a "universal affirmative," it is enough to prove its contradictory, which is a "particular negative." (I must pause for a digression on Logic, and especially on Ladies' Logic. The universal affirmative "everybody says he's a duck" is crushed instantly by proving the particular negative "Peter says he's a goose," which is equivalent to "Peter does not say he's a duck." And the universal negative "nobody calls on her" is well met by the particular affirmative "I called yesterday." In short, either of two contradictories disproves the other: and the moral is that, since a particular proposition is much more easily proved than a universal one, it is the wisest course, in arguing with a Lady, to limit one's own assertions to "particulars," and leave her to prove the "universal" contradictory, if she can. You will thus generally secure a logical victory: a practical victory is not to be hoped for, since she can always fall back upon the crushing remark "that has nothing to do with it!"—a move for which Man has not yet discovered any satisfactory answer. Now let us return to Balbus.) Here is my "particular negative," on which to test his rule. Suppose the two recorded luncheons to have been "2 buns, one queen-cake, 2 sausage-rolls, and a bottle of Zoëdone: total, one-and-ninepence," and "one bun, 2 queen-cakes, a sausage-roll, and a bottle of Zoëdone: total, one-and-fourpence." And suppose Clara's unknown luncheon to have been "3 buns, one queen-cake, one sausage-roll, and 2 bottles of Zoëdone:" while the two little sisters had been indulging in "8 buns, 4 queen-cakes, 2 sausage-rolls, and 6 bottles of Zoëdone." (Poor souls, how thirsty they must have been!) If Balbus will kindly try this by his principle of "two assumptions," first assuming that a bun is 1d. and a queen-cake 2d., and then that a bun is 3d. and a queen-cake 3d., he will bring out the other two luncheons, on each assumption, as "one-and-nine-pence" and "four-and-ten-pence" respectively, which harmony of results, he will say, "shows that the answers are correct." And yet, as a matter of fact, the buns were 2d. each, the queen-cakes 3d., the sausage-rolls 6d., and the Zoëdone 2d. a bottle: so that Clara's third luncheon had cost

79

one-and-sevenpence, and her thirsty friends had spent four-and-fourpence!

Another remark of Balbus I will quote and discuss: for I think that it also may yield a moral for some of my readers. He says "it is the same thing in substance whether in solving this problem we use words and call it Arithmetic, or use letters and signs and call it Algebra." Now this does not appear to me a correct description of the two methods: the Arithmetical method is that of "synthesis" only; it goes from one known fact to another, till it reaches its goal: whereas the Algebraical method is that of "analysis": it begins with the goal, symbolically represented, and so goes backwards, dragging its veiled victim with it, till it has reached the full daylight of known facts, in which it can tear off the veil and say "I know you!"

Take an illustration. Your house has been broken into and robbed, and you appeal to the policeman who was on duty that night. "Well, Mum, I did see a chap getting out over your garden-wall: but I was a good bit off, so I didn't chase him, like. I just cut down the short way to the Chequers, and who should I meet but Bill Sykes, coming full split round the corner. So I just ups and says 'My lad, you're wanted.' That's all I says. And he says 'I'll go along quiet, Bobby,' he says, 'without the darbies,' he says." There's your Arithmetical policeman. Now try the other method. "I seed somebody a running, but he was well gone or ever I got nigh the place. So I just took a look round in the garden. And I noticed the foot-marks, where the chap had come right across your flower-beds. They was good big foot-marks sure-ly. And I noticed as the left foot went down at the heel, ever so much deeper than the other. And I says to myself 'The chap's been a big hulking chap: and he goes lame on his left foot.' And I rubs my hand on the wall where he got over, and there was soot on it, and no mistake. So I says to myself 'Now where can I light on a big man, in the chimbley-sweep line, what's lame of one foot?' And I flashes up permiscuous: and I says 'It's Bill Sykes!' says I." There is your Algebraical policeman—a higher intellectual type, to my thinking, than the other.

Little Jack's solution calls for a word of praise, as he has written out what really is an algebraical proof in words, without representing any of his facts as equations. If it is all his own, he will make a good algebraist in the time to come. I beg to thank Simple Susan for some kind words of sympathy, to the same effect as those received from Old Cat.

Hecla and Martreb are the only two who have used a method certain either to produce the answer, or else to prove it impossible: so they must share between them the highest honours.

CLASS LIST

I

Hecla.
Martreb.

II

§ 1 (2 steps).

Adelaide.
Clifton C....
E. K. C.
Guy.
L'Inconnu.
Little Jack.
Nil desperandum.
Simple Susan.
Yellow-Hammer.
Woolly One.

§ 2 (3 steps).

A. A.

A Christmas Carol.
Afternoon Tea.
An appreciative Schoolma'am.
Baby.
Balbus.
Bog-Oak.
The Red Queen.
Wall-flower.

§ 3 (4 steps).

Hawthorn.
Joram.
S. S. G.

§ 4 (5 steps).

A Stepney Coach.

§ 5 (6 steps).

Bay Laurel.
Bradshaw of the Future.

§ 6 (9 steps).

Old King Cole.

§ 7 (14 steps).

Theseus.

ANSWERS TO CORRESPONDENTS

I have received several letters on the subjects of Knots II. and VI., which lead me to think some further explanation desirable.

In Knot II., I had intended the numbering of the houses to begin at one corner of the Square, and this was assumed by most, if not all, of the competitors. Trojanus however says "assuming, in default of any information, that the street enters the square in the middle of each side, it may be supposed that the numbering begins at a street." But surely the other is the more natural assumption?

In Knot VI., the first Problem was of course a mere jeu de mots, whose presence I thought excusable in a series of Problems whose aim is to entertain rather than to instruct: but it has not escaped the contemptuous criticisms of two of my correspondents, who seem to think that Apollo is in duty bound to keep his bow always on the stretch. Neither of them has guessed it: and this is true human nature. Only the other day—the 31st of September, to be quite exact—I met my old friend Brown, and gave him a riddle I had just heard. With one great effort of his colossal mind, Brown guessed it. "Right!" said I. "Ah," said he, "it's very neat—very neat. And it isn't an answer that would occur to everybody. Very neat indeed." A few yards further on, I fell in with Smith and to him I propounded the same riddle. He frowned over it for a minute, and then gave it up. Meekly I faltered out the answer. "A poor thing, sir!" Smith growled, as he turned away. "A very poor thing! I wonder you care to repeat such rubbish!" Yet Smith's mind is, if possible, even more colossal than Brown's.

The second Problem of Knot VI. is an example in ordinary Double Rule of Three, whose essential feature is that the result depends on the variation of several elements, which are so related to it that, if all but one be constant, it varies as that one: hence, if none be constant, it varies as their product. Thus, for example, the cubical contents of a rectangular tank vary as its length, if breadth and depth be constant, and so on; hence, if none be constant, it varies as the product of the length, breadth, and depth.

When the result is not thus connected with the varying elements, the Problem ceases to be Double Rule of Three and often becomes one of great complexity.

To illustrate this, let us take two candidates for a prize, A and B, who are to compete in French, German, and Italian:

(a) Let it be laid down that the result is to depend on their relative knowledge of each subject, so that, whether their marks, for French, be "1, 2" or "100, 200," the result will be the same: and let it also be laid down that, if they get equal marks on 2 papers, the final marks are to have the same ratio as those of the 3rd paper. This is a case of ordinary Double Rule of Three. We multiply A's 3 marks together, and do the same for B. Note that, if A gets a single "0," his final mark is "0," even if he gets full marks for 2 papers while B gets only one mark for each paper. This of course would be very unfair on A, though a correct solution under the given conditions.

(b) The result is to depend, as before, on relative knowledge; but French is to have twice as much weight as German or Italian. This is an unusual form of question. I should be inclined to say "the resulting ratio is to be nearer to the French ratio than if we multiplied as in (a), and so much nearer that it would be necessary to use the other multipliers twice to produce the same result as in (a):" e.g. if the French Ratio were 2/10, and the others 2/9, 1/9 so that the ultimate ratio, by method (a), would be 2/45, I should multiply instead by 2/3, 1/3, giving the result, 1/3 which is nearer to 2/10 than if he had used method (a).

(c) The result is to depend on actual amount of knowledge of the 3 subjects collectively. Here we have to ask two questions. (1) What is to be the "unit" (i.e. "standard to measure by") in each subject? (2) Are these units to be of equal, or unequal value? The usual "unit" is the knowledge shown by answering the whole paper correctly; calling this "100," all lower amounts are represented by numbers

84

between "0" and "100." Then, if these units are to be of equal value, we simply add A's 3 marks together, and do the same for B.

(d) The conditions are the same as (c), but French is to have double weight. Here we simply double the French marks, and add as before.

(e) French is to have such weight, that, if other marks be equal, the ultimate ratio is to be that of the French paper, so that a "0" in this would swamp the candidate: but the other two subjects are only to affect the result collectively, by the amount of knowledge shown, the two being reckoned of equal value. Here I should add A's German and Italian marks together, and multiply by his French mark.

But I need not go on: the problem may evidently be set with many varying conditions, each requiring its own method of solution. The Problem in Knot VI. was meant to belong to variety (a), and to make this clear, I inserted the following passage:

"Usually the competitors differ in one point only. Thus, last year, Fifi and Gogo made the same number of scarves in the trial week, and they were equally light; but Fifi's were twice as warm as Gogo's, and she was pronounced twice as good."

What I have said will suffice, I hope, as an answer to Balbus, who holds that (a) and (c) are the only possible varieties of the problem, and that to say "We cannot use addition, therefore we must be intended to use multiplication," is "no more illogical than, from knowledge that one was not born in the night, to infer that he was born in the daytime"; and also to Fifee, who says "I think a little more consideration will show you that our 'error of adding the proportional numbers together for each candidate instead of multiplying' is no error at all." Why, even if addition had been the right method to use, not one of the writers (I speak from memory) showed any consciousness of the necessity of fixing a "unit" for each subject. "No error at all!" They were positively steeped in error!

One correspondent (I do not name him, as the communication is not quite friendly in tone) writes thus:—"I wish to add, very respectfully, that I think it would be in better taste if you were to abstain from the very trenchant expressions which you are accustomed to indulge in when criticising the answer. That such a tone must not be" ("be not"?) "agreeable to the persons concerned who have made mistakes may possibly have no great weight with you, but I hope you will feel that it would be as well not to employ it, unless you are quite certain of being correct yourself." The only instances the writer gives of the "trenchant expressions" are "hapless" and "malefactors." I beg to assure him (and any others who may need the assurance: I trust there are none) that all such words have been used in jest, and with no idea that they could possibly annoy any one, and that I sincerely regret any annoyance I may have thus inadvertently given. May I hope that in future they will recognise the distinction between severe language used in sober earnest, and the "words of unmeant bitterness," which Coleridge has alluded to in that lovely passage beginning "A little child, a limber elf"? If the writer will refer to that passage, or to the preface to "Fire, Famine, and Slaughter," he will find the distinction, for which I plead, far better drawn out than I could hope to do in any words of mine.

The writer's insinuation that I care not how much annoyance I give to my readers I think it best to pass over in silence; but to his concluding remark I must entirely demur. I hold that to use language likely to annoy any of my correspondents would not be in the least justified by the plea that I was "quite certain of being correct." I trust that the knot-untiers and I are not on such terms as those!

I beg to thank G. B. for the offer of a puzzle—which, however, is too like the old one "Make four 9's into 100."

ANSWERS TO KNOT VIII

§ 1. The Pigs

Problem.—Place twenty-four pigs in four sties so that, as you go round and round, you may always find the number in each sty nearer to ten than the number in the last.

Answer.—Place 8 pigs in the first sty, 10 in the second, nothing in the third, and 6 in the fourth: 10 is nearer ten than 8; nothing is nearer ten than 10; 6 is nearer ten than nothing; and 8 is nearer ten than 6.

This problem is noticed by only two correspondents. Balbus says "it certainly cannot be solved mathematically, nor do I see how to solve it by any verbal quibble." Nolens Volens makes Her Radiancy change the direction of going round; and even then is obliged to add "the pigs must be carried in front of her"!

§ 2. The Grurmstipths

Problem.—Omnibuses start from a certain point, both ways, every 15 minutes. A traveller, starting on foot along with one of them, meets one in 12½ minutes: when will he be overtaken by one?

Answer.—In 6¼ minutes.

Solution.—Let "a" be the distance an omnibus goes in 15 minutes, and "x" the distance from the starting-point to where the traveller is overtaken. Since the omnibus met is due at the starting-point in 2½ minutes, it goes in that time as far as the traveller walks in 12½; i.e. it goes 5 times as fast. Now the overtaking omnibus is "a" behind the traveller when he starts, and therefore goes "a + x" while he goes "x." Hence a + x = 5x; i.e. 4x = a, and x = a/4. This distance would be

87

traversed by an omnibus in 15/4 minutes, and therefore by the traveller in 5 × 15/4. Hence he is overtaken in 18¾ minutes after starting, i.e. in 6¼ minutes after meeting the omnibus.

Four answers have been received, of which two are wrong. Dinah Mite rightly states that the overtaking omnibus reached the point where they met the other omnibus 5 minutes after they left, but wrongly concludes that, going 5 times as fast, it would overtake them in another minute. The travellers are 5-minutes-walk ahead of the omnibus, and must walk 1-4th of this distance farther before the omnibus overtakes them, which will be 1-5th of the distance traversed by the omnibus in the same time: this will require 1¼ minutes more. Nolens Volens tries it by a process like "Achilles and the Tortoise." He rightly states that, when the overtaking omnibus leaves the gate, the travellers are 1-5th of "a" ahead, and that it will take the omnibus 3 minutes to traverse this distance; "during which time" the travellers, he tells us, go 1-15th of "a" (this should be 1-25th). The travellers being now 1-15th of "a" ahead, he concludes that the work remaining to be done is for the travellers to go 1-60th of "a," while the omnibus goes 1-12th. The principle is correct, and might have been applied earlier.

CLASS LIST

I

Balbus.
Delta.

ANSWERS TO KNOT IX

§ 1. The Buckets

Problem.—Lardner states that a solid, immersed in a fluid, displaces an amount equal to itself in bulk. How can this be true of a small bucket floating in a larger one?

Solution.—Lardner means, by "displaces," "occupies a space which might be filled with water without any change in the surroundings." If the portion of the floating bucket, which is above the water, could be annihilated, and the rest of it transformed into water, the surrounding water would not change its position: which agrees with Lardner's statement.

Five answers have been received, none of which explains the difficulty arising from the well-known fact that a floating body is the same weight as the displaced fluid. Hecla says that "only that portion of the smaller bucket which descends below the original level of the water can be properly said to be immersed, and only an equal bulk of water is displaced." Hence, according to Hecla, a solid, whose weight was equal to that of an equal bulk of water, would not float till the whole of it was below "the original level" of the water: but, as a matter of fact, it would float as soon as it was all under water. Magpie says the fallacy is "the assumption that one body can displace another from a place where it isn't," and that Lardner's assertion is incorrect, except when the containing vessel "was originally full to the brim." But the question of floating depends on the present state of things, not on past history. Old King Cole takes the same view as Hecla. Tympanum and Vindex assume that "displaced" means "raised above its original level," and merely explain how it comes to pass that the water, so raised, is less in bulk than the immersed portion of bucket, and thus land themselves—or rather set themselves floating—in the same boat as Hecla.

I regret that there is no Class-list to publish for this Problem.

§ 2. Balbus' Essay

Problem.—Balbus states that if a certain solid be immersed in a certain vessel of water, the water will rise through a series of distances, two inches, one inch, half an inch, &c., which series has no end. He concludes that the water will rise without limit. Is this true?

Solution.—No. This series can never reach 4 inches, since, however many terms we take, we are always short of 4 inches by an amount equal to the last term taken.

Three answers have been received—but only two seem to me worthy of honours.

Tympanum says that the statement about the stick "is merely a blind, to which the old answer may well be applied, solvitur ambulando, or rather mergendo." I trust Tympanum will not test this in his own person, by taking the place of the man in Balbus' Essay! He would infallibly be drowned.

Old King Cole rightly points out that the series, 2, 1, &c., is a decreasing Geometrical Progression: while Vindex rightly identifies the fallacy as that of "Achilles and the Tortoise."

CLASS LIST

I

Old King Cole.
Vindex.

§ 3. The Garden

Problem.—An oblong garden, half a yard longer than wide, consists entirely of a gravel-walk, spirally arranged, a yard wide and 3,630 yards long. Find the dimensions of the garden.

Answer.—60, 60½.

Solution.—The number of yards and fractions of a yard traversed in walking along a straight piece of walk, is evidently the same as the number of square-yards and fractions of a square-yard, contained in that piece of walk: and the distance, traversed in passing through a square-yard at a corner, is evidently a yard. Hence the area of the garden is 3,630 square-yards: i.e., if x be the width, x (x + ½) = 3,630. Solving this Quadratic, we find x = 60. Hence the dimensions are 60, 60½.

Twelve answers have been received—seven right and five wrong.

C. G. L., Nabob, Old Crow, and Tympanum assume that the number of yards in the length of the path is equal to the number of square-yards in the garden. This is true, but should have been proved. But each is guilty of darker deeds. C. G. L.'s "working" consists of dividing 3,630 by 60. Whence came this divisor, oh Segiel? Divination? Or was it a dream? I fear this solution is worth nothing. Old Crow's is shorter, and so (if possible) worth rather less. He says the answer "is at once seen to be 60 × 60½"! Nabob's calculation is short, but "as rich as a Nabob" in error. He says that the square root of 3,630, multiplied by 2, equals the length plus the breadth. That is 60.25 × 2 = 120½. His first assertion is only true of a square garden. His second is irrelevant, since 60.25 is not the square-root of 3,630! Nay, Bob, this will not do! Tympanum says that, by extracting the square-root of 3,630, we get 60 yards with a remainder of 30/60, or half-a-yard, which we add so as to make the oblong 60 × 60½. This is very terrible: but worse remains behind. Tympanum proceeds thus:—"But why should there be the half-yard at all? Because without it there would be no space at all for flowers. By means of it, we find reserved in the very centre a small plot of ground, two yards long by half-a-yard wide, the only space not occupied by walk." But Balbus expressly said that the walk "used up the whole of the area." Oh, Tympanum! My tympa is exhausted: my brain is num! I can say no more.

Hecla indulges, again and again, in that most fatal of all habits in computation—the making two mistakes which cancel each other. She takes x as the width of the garden, in yards, and x + ½ as its length, and makes her first "coil" the sum of x½, x½, x-1, x-1, i.e. 4x-3: but the fourth term should be x-1½, so that her first coil is ½ a yard too long. Her second coil is the sum of x-2½, x-2½, x-3, x-3: here the first term should be x-2 and the last x-3½: these two mistakes cancel, and this coil is therefore right. And the same thing is true of every other coil but the last, which needs an extra half-yard to reach the end of the path: and this exactly balances the mistake in the first coil. Thus the sum total of the coils comes right though the working is all wrong.

Of the seven who are right, Dinah Mite, Janet, Magpie, and Taffy make the same assumption as C. G. L. and Co. They then solve by a Quadratic. Magpie also tries it by Arithmetical Progression, but fails to notice that the first and last "coils" have special values.

Alumnus Etonæ attempts to prove what C. G. L. assumes by a particular instance, taking a garden 6 by 5½. He ought to have proved it generally: what is true of one number is not always true of others. Old King Cole solves it by an Arithmetical Progression. It is right, but too lengthy to be worth as much as a Quadratic.

Vindex proves it very neatly, by pointing out that a yard of walk measured along the middle represents a square yard of garden, "whether we consider the straight stretches of walk or the square yards at the angles, in which the middle line goes half a yard in one direction and then turns a right angle and goes half a yard in another direction."

CLASS LIST

I

Vindex.

II

Alumnus Etonæ.
Old King Cole.

III

Dinah Mite.
Janet.
Magpie.
Taffy.

§ 1. The Chelsea Pensioners

Problem.—If 70 per cent. have lost an eye, 75 per cent. an ear, 80 per cent. an arm, 85 per cent. a leg: what percentage, at least, must have lost all four?

Answer.—Ten.

Solution.—(I adopt that of Polar Star, as being better than my own). Adding the wounds together, we get 70 + 75 + 80 + 85 = 310, among 100 men; which gives 3 to each, and 4 to 10 men. Therefore the least percentage is 10.

Nineteen answers have been received. One is "5," but, as no working is given with it, it must, in accordance with the rule, remain "a deed without a name." Janet makes it "35 and 2⁄10ths." I am sorry she has misunderstood the question, and has supposed that those who had lost an ear were 75 per cent. of those who had lost an eye; and so on. Of course, on this supposition, the percentages must all be multiplied together. This she has done correctly, but I can give her no honours, as I do not think the question will fairly bear her interpretation, Three Score and Ten makes it "19 and 2⁄8ths." Her solution has given me—I will not say "many anxious days and sleepless nights," for I wish to be strictly truthful, but—some trouble in making any sense at all of it. She makes the number of "pensioners wounded once" to be 310 ("per cent.," I suppose!): dividing by 4, she gets 77 and a half as "average percentage:" again dividing by 4, she gets 19 and 2⁄8ths as "percentage wounded four times." Does she suppose wounds of different kinds to "absorb" each other, so to speak? Then, no doubt, the data are equivalent to 77 pensioners with one wound each, and a half-pensioner with a half-wound. And does she then suppose these concentrated wounds to be transferable, so that 2⁄4ths of these unfortunates can obtain perfect health by handing over their wounds to the remaining 1⁄4th? Granting these suppositions, her answer is right; or rather, if the question had been "A road is covered with one inch of gravel, along 77 and a half per cent. of it. How much of it could be covered 4 inches deep with the same material?" her answer would have been right. But alas, that wasn't the question! Delta makes some most amazing assumptions: "let every one who has not lost an eye have lost an ear," "let every one who has not lost both eyes and ears have lost an arm." Her ideas of a battle-field are grim indeed. Fancy a warrior who would continue fighting after losing both eyes, both ears, and both arms! This is a case which she (or "it?") evidently considers possible.

Next come eight writers who have made the unwarrantable assumption that, because 70 per cent. have lost an eye, therefore 30 per cent. have not lost one, so that they have both eyes. This is illogical. If you give me a bag containing 100 sovereigns, and if in an hour I come to you (my face not beaming with gratitude nearly so much as when I received the bag) to say "I am sorry to tell you that 70 of these sovereigns are bad," do I thereby guarantee the other 30 to be good? Perhaps I have not tested them yet. The sides of this illogical octagon are as follows, in alphabetical order:— Algernon Bray, Dinah Mite, G. S. C., Jane E., J. D. W., Magpie (who makes the delightful remark "therefore 90 per cent. have two of something," recalling to one's memory that fortunate monarch, with whom Xerxes was so much pleased that "he gave him ten of everything!"), S. S. G., and Tokio.

Bradshaw of the Future and T. R. do the question in a piecemeal fashion—on the principle that the 70 per cent. and the 75 per cent., though commenced at opposite ends of the 100, must overlap by at least 45 per cent.; and so on. This is quite correct working, but not, I think, quite the best way of doing it.

The other five competitors will, I hope, feel themselves sufficiently glorified by being placed in the first class, without my composing a Triumphal Ode for each!

I

Old Cat.
Old Hen.
Polar Star.
Simple Susan.
White Sugar.

II

Bradshaw of the Future.
T. R.

III

Algernon Bray.
Dinah Mite.
G. S. C.
Jane E.
J. D. W.
Magpie.
S. S. G.
Tokio.

§ 2. Change of Day

I must postpone, sine die, the geographical problem—partly because I have not yet received the statistics I am hoping for, and partly because I am myself so entirely puzzled by it; and when an examiner is himself dimly hovering between a second class and a third how is he to decide the position of others?

§ 3. The Sons' Ages

Problem.—"At first, two of the ages are together equal to the third. A few years afterwards, two of them are together double of the third. When the number of years since the first occasion is two-thirds of the sum of the ages on that occasion, one age is 21. What are the other two?

Answer.—"15 and 18."

Solution.—Let the ages at first be x, y, (x + y). Now, if a + b = 2c, then (a-n) + (b-n) = 2(c-n), whatever be the value of n. Hence the second relationship, if ever true, was always true. Hence it was true at first. But it cannot be true that x and y are together double of (x + y). Hence it must be true of (x + y), together with x or y; and it does not matter which we take. We assume, then, (x + y) + x = 2y; i.e. y = 2x. Hence the three ages were, at first, x, 2x, 3x; and the number of years, since that time is two-thirds of 6x, i.e. is 4x. Hence the present ages are 5x, 6x, 7x. The ages are clearly integers, since this is only "the year when one of my sons comes of age." Hence 7x = 21, x = 3, and the other ages are 15, 18.

Eighteen answers have been received. One of the writers merely asserts that the first occasion was 12 years ago, that the ages were then 9, 6, and 3; and that on the second occasion they were 14, 11, and 8! As a Roman father, I ought to withhold the name of the rash writer; but respect for age makes me break the rule: it is Three Score and Ten. Jane E. also asserts that the ages at first were 9, 6, 3: then she calculates the present ages, leaving the second occasion unnoticed. Old Hen is nearly as bad; she "tried various numbers till I found one that fitted all the conditions"; but merely scratching up the earth, and pecking about, is not the way to solve a problem, oh venerable bird! And close after Old Hen prowls, with hungry eyes, Old Cat, who calmly assumes, to begin with, that the son who comes of age is the eldest. Eat your bird, Puss, for you will get nothing from me!

There are yet two zeroes to dispose of. Minerva assumes that, on every occasion, a son comes of age; and that it is only such a son who is "tipped with gold." Is it wise thus to interpret "now, my boys, calculate your ages, and you shall have the money"? Bradshaw of the Future says "let" the ages at first be 9, 6, 3, then assumes that the second occasion was 6 years afterwards, and on these baseless assumptions brings out the right answers. Guide future travellers, an thou wilt: thou art no Bradshaw for this Age!

Of those who win honours, the merely "honourable" are two. Dinah Mite ascertains (rightly) the relationship between the three ages at first, but then assumes one of them to be "6," thus making the rest of her solution tentative. M. F. C. does the algebra all right up to the conclusion that the present ages are $5z$, $6z$, and $7z$; it then assumes, without giving any reason, that $7z = 21$.

Of the more honourable, Delta attempts a novelty—to discover which son comes of age by elimination: it assumes, successively, that it is the middle one, and that it is the youngest; and in each case it apparently brings out an absurdity. Still, as the proof contains the following bit of algebra, "$63 = 7x + 4y$; $\therefore 21 = x + 4$ sevenths of y," I trust it will admit that its proof is not quite conclusive. The rest of its work is good. Magpie betrays the deplorable tendency of her tribe—to appropriate any stray conclusion she comes across, without having any strict logical right to it. Assuming A, B, C, as the ages at first, and D as the number of the years that have elapsed since then, she finds (rightly) the 3 equations, $2A = B$, $C = B + A$, $D = 2B$. She then says "supposing that $A = 1$, then $B = 2$, $C = 3$, and $D = 4$. Therefore for A, B, C, D, four numbers are wanted which shall be to each other as 1:2:3:4." It is in the "therefore" that I detect the unconscientiousness of this bird. The conclusion is true, but this is only because the equations are "homogeneous" (i.e. having one "unknown" in each term), a fact which I strongly suspect had not been grasped—I beg pardon, clawed—by her. Were I to lay this little pitfall, "$A + 1 = B$, $B + 1 = C$; supposing $A = 1$, then $B = 2$ and $C = 3$. Therefore for A, B, C, three numbers are wanted which shall be to one another as 1:2:3," would you not flutter down into it, oh Magpie, as amiably as a Dove? Simple Susan is anything but simple to me. After ascertaining that the 3 ages at first are as 3:2:1, she says "then, as two-thirds of their sum, added to one of them, = 21, the sum cannot exceed 30, and consequently the highest cannot exceed 15." I suppose her (mental) argument is something like this:—"two-thirds of sum, + one age, = 21; ∴ sum, + 3 halves of one age, = 31 and a half. But 3 halves of one age cannot be less than 1 and-a-half (here I perceive that Simple Susan would on no account present a guinea to a new-born baby!) hence the sum cannot exceed 30." This is ingenious, but her proof, after that, is (as she candidly admits) "clumsy and roundabout." She finds that there are 5 possible sets of ages, and eliminates four of them. Suppose that, instead of 5, there had been 5 million possible sets? Would Simple Susan have courageously ordered in the necessary gallon of ink and ream of paper?

The solution sent in by C. R. is, like that of Simple Susan, partly tentative, and so does not rise higher than being Clumsily Right.

Among those who have earned the highest honours, Algernon Bray solves the problem quite correctly, but adds that there is nothing to exclude the supposition that all the ages were fractional. This would make the number of answers infinite. Let me meekly protest that I never intended my readers to devote the rest of their lives to writing out answers! E. M. Rix points out that, if fractional ages be admissible, any one of the three sons might be the one "come of age"; but she rightly rejects this supposition on the ground that it would make the problem indeterminate. White Sugar is the only one who has detected an oversight of mine: I had forgotten the possibility (which of course ought to be allowed for) that the son, who came of age that year, need not have done so by that day, so that he might be only 20. This gives a second solution, viz., 20, 24, 28. Well said, pure Crystal! Verily, thy "fair discourse hath been as sugar"!

CLASS LIST

I

Algernon Bray.
An Old Fogey.
E. M. Rix.
G. S. C.
S. S. G.
Tokio.
T. R.
White Sugar.

II

C. R.
Delta.
Magpie.
Simple Susan.

III

Dinah Mite.
M. F. C.

I have received more than one remonstrance on my assertion, in the Chelsea Pensioners' problem, that it was illogical to assume, from the datum "70 p. c. have lost an eye," that 30 p. c. have not. Algernon Bray states, as a parallel case, "suppose Tommy's father gives him 4 apples, and he eats one of them, how many has he left?" and says "I think we are justified in answering, 3." I think so too. There is no "must" here, and the data are evidently meant to fix the answer exactly: but, if the question were set me "how many must he have left?", I should understand the data to be that his father gave him 4 at least, but may have given him more.

I take this opportunity of thanking those who have sent, along with their answers to the Tenth Knot, regrets that there are no more Knots to come, or petitions that I should recall my resolution to bring them to an end. I am most grateful for their kind words; but I think it wisest to end what, at best, was but a lame attempt. "The stretched metre of an antique song" is beyond my compass; and my puppets were neither distinctly in my life (like those I now address), nor yet (like Alice and the Mock Turtle) distinctly out of it. Yet let me at least fancy, as I lay down the pen, that I carry with me into my silent life, dear reader, a farewell smile from your unseen face, and a kindly farewell pressure from your unfelt hand! And so, good night! Parting is such sweet sorrow, that I shall say "good night!" till it be morrow.

THE END

www.ingramcontent.com/pod-product-compliance
Lightning Source LLC
Chambersburg PA
CBHW011440170626
46807CB00008B/3252